BIRD WITH A BROKEN WING

Bertie has tomboyish ways and champions defenceless things, like a bird with a broken wing. But her youthful exterior hides a woman's heart, which craves for love. She envies the feminine Marcia, so admired by Bill Newbury. Bertie discovers that — like the injured birds — a man, too, can be maimed by his relationships and may need nursing and care. Yet is it enough to be needed? Bertie wants to be loved — something which has always escaped her and appears likely to elude her still.

J. L. SOMERS

BIRD WITH A BROKEN WING

Complete and Unabridged

LINFORD
Leicester

First published in Great Britain in 1966 by
Robert Hale Limited
London

First Linford Edition
published 2006
by arrangement with
Robert Hale Limited
London

British Library CIP Data

Somers, J. L.
  Bird with a broken wing.—Large print ed.—
Linford romance library
1. Love stories
2. Large type books
I. Title
823.9′14 [F]

ISBN 1–84617–222–5

Published by
F. A. Thorpe (Publishing)
Anstey, Leicestershire

Set by Words & Graphics Ltd.
Anstey, Leicestershire
Printed and bound in Great Britain by
T. J. International Ltd., Padstow, Cornwall

This book is printed on acid-free paper

FOR
VERA EVANS

PART ONE

PART ONE

1

One or two stunted firs flanked the sandy track and, seeing a cone in her path, she began to kick it idly along. She was thinking of her next term. She would work hard. She must reach A level when she took her G.C.E. in July. Then there would be college — a magical word. College — a magical world.

A sudden delighted little yap broke into her thoughts and a small black and white shape hurtled past her legs to pounce on the fir-cone she had just sent flying. Then, its stumpy tail wagging, a terrier came back to drop the missile at her feet.

She chuckled and gave another kick, her brown eyes lighting with amusement to see the little dog go chasing off again in pursuit of the airborne cone. She glanced back, expecting to find the animal's owner was somewhere near, but no one was in sight.

The path curved and she went down a stony incline and so on to an open common. There was no sign of any other living creature except herself and the terrier. She stood looking out across the brown heathland, trying to imagine it in summertime with the heather in bloom.

When at last she turned to go back, the dog, which had accompanied her all the way, began to return with her. It frisked ahead, then turned and frolicked around her before racing on excitedly again in front. She was walking briskly and decided to skirt the knoll over which she had so recently climbed. She looked away towards the left where the sky was a blaze of red, streaked with horizontal black clouds. But she paused for no more than a moment for, all at once, there came a most awful commotion.

The small terrier was contending for right of way on the narrow path with a dog much bigger than itself. The girl gave a shrill whistle but the animal did not heed. Then a man appeared. He was outlined briefly against the sky above her. He called, 'Rusty! Rusty!'

But the bigger dog took no notice either. The girl rushed forward, grabbing for the little black and white terrier among the growling, quickly-moving mass of heads and legs that might have belonged to six dogs instead of two!

Poor little chap — he didn't stand much chance against this great brute . . . she missed and grabbed again.

'Dafty!' the man shouted. 'Get back. You will get yourself bitten.' With the crook of his stick he hooked Rusty's collar and then she managed to get hold of the smaller dog.

As she picked him up she saw that his paw was torn and bleeding. The man said, 'My name is Newbury — Bill Newbury — in case anything goes wrong with your tyke.' He managed to get a lot of scorn into that last word, while hostility bristled in his voice and the lift of his broad shoulders. 'I live in Turbary Grange — on the corner of the lane. I don't suppose the pup'll be any the worse after a couple of days, but you'd better wash that paw when you get home.'

'I suppose a dog owner always thinks the common belongs to his own particular pet,' the girl said hotly. 'Well, this little thing isn't mine, but I'm not going to see it killed by your great brute.'

'Not yours!' he exclaimed. 'Well, I thought it looked a bit familiar. That's Dud Lambourne's mongrel, isn't it?'

'I don't know whose it is. It has followed me a long way. I was wondering what I was going to do with it.'

She fondled the small dog's ears. The bigger animal, held firmly by the man, stood quivering restlessly. She asked, 'What was the name you said?'

The hostility had died from Bill Newbury's face, and he said, 'Dud

Lambourne. You're a stranger here, aren't you?'

She nodded. 'We only arrived on Friday.'

'Then you wouldn't have heard of Dud. He's a bit slow.'

'Where does he live? I'll have to take his dog back to him.'

'White Farm — it's over behind the church.'

'That must be near us,' she said. 'I'll be moving. I must get this small casualty seen to.'

'What is your name?' Bill asked.

'Bertie Shefford.'

'Bertie — that's not the real one,' he said.

'No.' She hesitated. Then she gave a little laugh. 'Alberta Patricia,' she told him, 'but do you imagine I *like* that mouthful?'

He grinned. 'I like Bertie better — it suits you.'

'You are thinking what most people do about me, that I'm more like a boy than a girl,' she said, and shrugged her bony shoulders.

'Perhaps you are,' he replied. 'Not many *girls* would be out of doors without a coat on a day as cold as this.'

With a sudden, unexpected movement he put his hand on the terrier's head, but his gaze was on the girl's face as he said, 'I'm afraid you might not have too warm a welcome at White Farm. Dud's mother is none too amiable. I would guess that Dud is out and she turned the dog loose on purpose. She hates the little creature.'

'What a shame!' She looked down at the terrier and then smiled. 'Thanks for the information — forewarned is forearmed,' she said.

As she began climbing up the stony incline to the lane Bertie glanced back. Bill Newbury was standing on the rise above her — tall, broad-shouldered, with a black unruly mop of hair. He waved his stick as she looked round and she waved back. Then he turned. She saw the stride of his long legs, the swing of his shoulders before he disappeared on the other side of the knoll.

He's good to look at, she thought.

She was carrying the little dog cradled in her arms and hurrying now as fast as she could but, nearing home, found she was overtaking an elderly man. He glanced round at her.

'Hullo,' he said. 'Perhaps you don't know, but I live in the house on the corner — next door to you.'

'Oh yes — on the other side of the lane. It's quite nice being in a corner house and having a side wicket so that you can get out the back . . . ' Rather reluctantly Bertie had dropped to his pace. It would be unneighbourly to rush on.

He was saying, 'I am so glad there are young folk in your house now — and I do hope we'll all be friends. My name is Fawley.'

Bertie told him that theirs was Shefford.

He said after a pause, 'Now I have a niece coming to stay with us and my wife is dreading it. She is not at all like you — but fluffy and very feminine, if her photos are anything to go by.'

Again he paused. 'My wife is rather ailing, you know, and can't imagine how we will ever entertain Marcia. I do hope you two girls will be friendly.'

Bertie laughed. He sounded so wistful — as though he were trying to sell her his last pair of cauliflowers in a market!

'I'm a friendly-making sort of person,' she assured him, 'but I'm not sure your niece will like *me* if she's 'fluffy'.'

She was glad when he turned in at his gate and she could hurry on into her own home. She explained to her family what had happened and then, looking up at her father, asked, 'Do you know this Dud Lambourne or his mother?'

Jack Shefford shook his head. He had come to Cordery to manage The Cosy, which was the general stores. He was holding the little dog while Bertie bathed the injured paw. Now he said, 'I've met a good many of the folk here, and heard scraps about others — but I'm sure I haven't heard the name Lambourne mentioned. Would you like me to come along when you take the dog back — seeing what Bill Newbury told you?'

'No, of course not,' she said chuckling. 'This woman is not an ogre — just 'none too amiable'.'

'By the way, I *do* know who Rusty's owner is. His father is Dr. Newbury — rather a gruff old bird, but all right underneath I guess.'

Bertie's small brother and sister, David and Nesta, were twins, and now they were crowding close to see the bandaging performed. Dorothy, who was eight, had looked up when her older sister came in and then gone on with the book she was reading.

The small creature's sides were heaving, but he submitted docilely to Bertie's doctoring.

'You won't be able to take him back tonight,' Mrs. Shefford remarked. 'It will soon be dark.'

'Oh, but I must,' the girl returned quickly, glancing out of the window. 'It's only quarter to four. It won't be really dark for ages.' She stood up, holding her hands towards her father so that he could give her the small dog.

As she carried it away from her home it kept lifting its head to give her chin a grateful lick. She took a path which led out from the back of the house through a small plantation of firs. Here another track ran at right angles and, as she paused, she caught sight of a white building not far to her left. That must be White Farm, yet it was in reality little more than a small-holding. As she went up a recently gravelled path, Bertie glanced curiously round.

The man who lived here was called 'Dud,' and she wondered if *he* worked the place. For anyone 'a bit slow' to have everything so trim would be a miracle. No, it was probably his father who did it all.

The flower beds which ran on either

side of the path were showing by a host of green spears that Spring was only just around the corner. Beyond the house were ploughed fields, while further still she could glimpse cows feeding in a grassy meadow.

Rather dubiously she knocked on the front door, waiting so long that she thought she was not to be answered. Then a small woman appeared. Somehow Bertie had been expecting a big female with straggling hair and a loud voice. So this neatly-aproned little person, with grey hair drawn into a tight bun at the back of her head, was a surprise.

Bertie said, 'I believe this dog belongs to you. I . . . '

'Not to me,' the woman interrupted. 'And it's been hurt, has it? You let the vet have it and put it to sleep. That's the best thing to do about *him*.'

'I can't do that,' Bertie exclaimed indignantly.

The woman waved impatient hands, and the little dog cowered against

Bertie's chest. 'Take it away, I say. Take it away.'

The door shut with a conclusive thud. There was nothing Bertie could do except leave. Heading towards the line of fir-trees, and walking briskly, she was soon out of sight of the house. It was getting really dusk now. She decided she must keep the small dog for the night and try to find its master in the morning.

Then she realised that someone was coming towards her. It was a young man and as he drew level the animal, which had been snuggled against her, began to wriggle and give excited little barks. She did not need to ask — this was Dud Lambourne. He reached out and took the small creature with gentle hands.

His eyes were questioning and he opened his mouth, but it was some moments before he managed to get out, 'H . . . he's hurt. Wh . . . what h . . . happened?'

To Bertie, so quick in speech, it was

painful to see this man stuttering out his words, but she did not show her pity. She answered him easily, telling him how the terrier had been attracted by her cone, of the fight on the common and her own first-aid. Only when she reached the end of her story did she pause. She hesitated to tell him of the reception his mother had given her.

To gain time she nodded at the little dog, asking, 'What is his name?'

Again he made an effort to speak and though the girl felt another surge of compassion, she would not let him see it. Her eyes met his and she smiled, 'Could I guess it?'

His eyes were brown, dark and soft — like silky bulrushes beside a stream, and all at once it was as though the sun came out, sending up a reflection from rippling water. His eyes danced and, pursing his lips, he began to whistle.

The girl's own eyes lit up merrily and as he brought the lilting melody to a stop she laughed, saying, 'Poor old Joe

— but this baby's not old!'

Then she sobered. 'I'm afraid poor Joe's paw is rather badly torn and will need looking after. I went to White Farm and your mother wanted me to take him to the vet . . . ' She saw his eyes cloud. Haltingly he stammered that he would have to get rid of Joe, that he had always wanted a dog but his mother said it 'muckied' the place — and now it was ill *she* would not look after it. She saw the way his hands tightened on the small body and how Joe reached up to lick at his face.

Bertie said quickly, 'Shall I look after him for you? I'm living at Medlars End. Perhaps you know it?' When he nodded she said, 'I'd love to have Joe — and you could see him when you liked — take him for a run or anything . . . ' She made the impulsive offer and then paused. 'That is, if my mother and father don't mind,' she added. Dad would say it was all right but she wasn't so sure of Mum. She might even think the same as Mrs. Lambourne . . .

'At any rate it will be O.K. while I'm on holiday this week,' she went on. 'Then I go back to school.' The dusk was rapidly deepening. Under the firs ahead it looked really dark, and she asked, 'Well, how about Joe? Will you trust him to me?'

He put the little dog into her arms, opened his mouth as though to say something and then, silently, abruptly turned away — but Bertie understood. He hadn't been able to put his gratitude into words.

As she went homewards she found herself thinking about him, comparing him with Bill Newbury. He was older than Bill, she guessed, perhaps twenty to Bill's eighteen years. And this week she herself had reached seventeen. That meant, if her guess was right, that the boy on the common was only a year older than she was. Bill . . . Bill . . . She liked the name. For the first time in her life Bertie was interested in a boy — and for the first time in her life she *did* mind that she 'ought to have been a boy herself' as she was so often told. She wished desperately, too, that she was not plain. It had never mattered before.

It was half past three the next afternoon when Bertie escaped. The hours had been filled with so many tasks. There had been housework and shopping — on which outing she had taken the twins. There had been Joe's paw to bathe, too. The dog was better and hopping about on three legs, but he was very listless. Bertie had expected he would rip off his bandage but he seemed not to have energy to bother with it. The only thing he wanted to do was to stay close to Bertie.

Already she was attached to the little creature, touched and amused by it — yet back of all her thoughts was an urgency to get out on the common again. It was Mrs. Shefford who at last gave the chance when she said, 'Bertie, slip up to the shop and get your Dad to give you some shillings for the gas. I'm sure it will go out when I have to light up — and it'll be dark very soon.'

Hastily Bertie made for the door. 'I won't be too long,' she promised, and went quietly out the back way. She wanted to be sure of getting away on her own, something that might have been impossible had the twins seen her going. Hurrying along a track which ran at the back of their house, she came to a narrow lane through fir trees, struck across the churchyard and so out to the road.

She glanced across the fields to her left and saw that mist hung low, looking like huge heaps of cotton wool banked against the further hedges. She had never seen anything like it, yet she was resolved to get out over the common, mist or no mist. When she reached the corner of the lane she hesitated only a moment, though she could not see far along it. Her brown eyes held a determined light as she turned purposefully into the track. Before long she was on top of the stony knoll from which yesterday she had been able to see a long way and where the wind had played around her, touching her cheeks with rough cold fingers.

This afternoon it was still nippy but there was no breeze and mist hung in the hollows — unmoving white balls of it that fascinated Bertie. They might have been huge snowballs.

She scrambled down the far side of the pebbly incline, straining her eyes ahead, glancing back — hoping all the time for the sight of a tall figure looming up towards her. But she was quite alone in the cold desolate world. She gave a laugh. 'Dafty! That's me all right. Fancy coming out here on the chance of seeing anyone! He's probably at work, anyway.'

She turned and began to retrace her steps, trying to shake off the disappointment that had closed over her like the cloying mist. It was darker this afternoon than the day before and with the sudden thought that her mother would begin to wonder where she was Bertie broke into a run. Her feet sent small pebbles flying behind her as she neared the corner of the lane. Then, from the side gate of Turbary Grange a large dog bounded towards her, and as it began to bark a voice called, 'Here, Rusty, here!'

Bertie stopped. Her hair was a tangled mop, her small plain face red from running. She looked in that moment a tomboy of about fourteen. She grinned as the dog reached her and said, 'Hullo, Rusty.'

The animal sniffed at her, walked round her, and she laughed. 'No, I haven't got Joe today,' she said. Then holding out her hand she demanded, 'Friends, Rusty?'

'Oh, he'll be friends all right today,' Bill Newbury remarked as he came towards her. 'How is Dud's pup?'

'He'll be better before too long,' she told the man, 'at least I hope so — I'm looking after him.'

'Oh! What happened?'

Bertie told him of her visit to White Farm and her subsequent meeting with

Joe's owner. 'Does everyone call him Dud — to his face?' she asked.

'Yes.'

'But . . . ' She was troubled by the memory of the other man's face — his eyes were so wistful, yet intelligent, and she was indignant all at once at the injustice of fate — which had cast these two in such different moulds. She was kicking at the ground with her shoe, but suddenly looked up at Bill.

'It's not fair,' she said. 'He's not a dud — and he's not slow, either, I'm sure. Just because he stammers to call him Dud . . . ' She was speaking hotly, jerkily, and her small face was very serious. Bill's eyes, as he returned her gaze, were alight with amusement. 'You are a champion for Dud! I have never heard anyone stick up for him before.'

'Then all you've heard is fun poked at him,' Bertie retorted indignantly. 'And I suppose you have laughed yourself. More's the shame on all of you — especially *you* who are a doctor's son.'

'So you have been making enquiries about me?' There was still amusement in his tone.

'No, my Dad happens to know your father a bit.'

'Your Dad?'

'He is manager of the general store and stationer's.'

'Oh yes . . . '

There was a pause before Bertie asked, 'Are you going to be a doctor?'

'Heaven forbid! I grew up in a doctor's house — lived with the horror of daily surgeries.'

'But . . . '

'Do you know what the word surgery means?' he broke in. 'Well, I'll tell you — it means coughs and groans and chatter — mostly about people's insides. It means a man sitting in a chair and listening to a succession of complaints about complaints — and writing out prescriptions for real and imaginary illnesses. Gosh — that's not a life I could stand. I'd rather lie straight down and die.'

'You wouldn't have to be a general practitioner like Dr. Newbury. You could be a surgeon or a specialist. Think how wonderful it would be, for instance, to give somebody back their sight.'

'No, nothing doing.'

'Are you an only son?'

'Yes.'

'Then I bet you are a disappointment to your father.'

'Um . . .'

'What *are* you going to be then?'

'A civil engineer, if that satisfies you, Curiosity Jane.'

Bertie flushed. 'I didn't intend to be inquisitive,' she said.

'I know — you were just interested — else I wouldn't have answered you,' he smiled.

Rusty had bounded off down the lane and Bill remarked, 'I'm just going over the heath. I believe you have *been* — and with no dog as an excuse, either!'

She laughed. 'I have lived in a town, and the common fascinates me. I'm going to love it always — I think especially when it is windy. I want to stand on top of that rise out there and have a shouting competition with the gale. And then when the heather is out . . . I'm longing for that. I have never seen any heather except in pictures.'

'You funny little thing!' Bill exclaimed. 'Ours is such an ordinary common. I never expected to hear anyone enthuse over it.' He glanced across the fields. 'That mist means snow,' he told her, 'and then the common will be out of bounds to you.'

He began to move after the impatient Rusty. 'So long,' he said. A moment later he had disappeared into the fog which seemed all at once much thicker. Bertie started to run again. It was nearly dark now and Mum would be really worrying — especially if the gas went out and there was no shilling to put in the meter. Hastily she made her way to The Cosy, collected the coins and began to race for home, relieved when she saw light coming from the window . . .

2

Bertie was almost disappointed that she woke next morning to the sound of pouring rain. She had been planning to show Bill Newbury that even snow could not keep her off the common. Her last thought the night before had been, 'I may not see him, but I'll be able to leave my footprints for him to see.'

But Bill's forecast had been wrong. The balls of mist had only heralded rain — torrential rain too. Bother! This meant staying indoors to amuse the twins.

She got out of bed and went across to the window. It was early but as she stood looking out she decided, 'What fun to be out in it!' She could put on a mac and her Wellingtons . . .

She crept quietly from her room, but on the landing she halted. From her parents' room came the sound of a moan and then her father's voice asking, 'Mother, what is it?'

'I feel so ill . . . '

All thought of going out was swept from Bertie's mind then, and during the next days she left the house hardly at all. Mrs. Shefford was really ill.

They fetched Dr. Newbury and he said, 'It's nervous exhaustion — just let her rest . . . '

Bertie assumed control of the house-keeping — her mother seemed unable to worry about anything. But inexorably the twelfth of January was approaching, and Bertie found herself watching the calendar with anxious eyes. What was going to happen if Mrs. Shefford was not well again by the time school opened?

She put that question to Dr. Newbury when he came one day. He was a thick-set man of medium height and it was easy to see why Bill had such thick black hair, but the older man had a brusque manner and he rarely smiled.

He said now, 'Your mother needs a long, long rest.'

'But she says she feels better — she insisted on getting up today.'

'Because she knows you will be going back to school — because she is making the effort to be all right by then, but . . .'

Bertie turned abruptly away from his serious gaze. She *had* to go back to school — even weeks could make a difference to her chances in the G.C.E. She opened the front door for the doctor, watched him as he walked away from her along the path, and she did not even remember that he was Bill's father. A challenge had been issued to her and all that day she tried to face it — always with the same result — I must go back to school — I must.

And when the twelfth arrived Mrs. Shefford got up for the first time since her collapse at her usual hour. Beginning to prepare the breakfast she said to Bertie, 'You'll have to hurry — don't forget you are not in town now.'

The girl hesitated. 'Mum, are you sure you are well enough to be left? There are the twins . . . '

'Don't fuss,' the woman returned, an irritable note in her voice. 'I'll be all right.'

Yet somehow all that day Bertie found it impossible to concentrate on her lessons and she finished the last part of her journey home that afternoon at a run. With a sense of foreboding she heard, as she opened the door, that both the twins were crying and Dorothy was saying, 'Oh, be quiet! Bertie will be here soon.'

'Dorothy, what is the matter?'

'Mum has fallen over and she won't speak to us . . . ' Dorothy herself was on the verge of tears.

Hastily Bertie went to her mother, who was lying on the living-room floor. She would have to get Dr. Newbury, was her first thought. And the children were still crying . . .

Then, in sudden relief, she heard the sound of footsteps on the path outside.

Hastily she went through the passage and pulled open the door.

'Oh — Dud!' she exclaimed. 'Oh, please come and help me.'

She had been feeling frightened and helpless — and very young. How she would ever have got through the next hour without Dud Lambourne she had no idea. He was so calm that his very presence seemed to help Bertie.

He said slowly, 'Send the children in next door. Mrs. Fawley will look after them while Mr. Fawley goes for the doctor.' He stumbled over many of the words, but Bertie did not really notice.

And then Dr. Newbury was there, looking grave and saying, 'Your mother must go into hospital. I'll ring for an ambulance right away. You'll go with her of course.'

Quietly Dud slipped away — off to tell Jack Shefford what had occurred, and it was her father who stayed the night at the hospital, having followed Bertie and her mother as soon as he heard what had happened.

For the first time in her life Bertie did not sleep all night. She could not forget the sight of her mother lying so still, nor her father's anxious face when she left them.

If anything happened to Mum . . . It was a thought which kept returning to Bertie — a thought which she refused to finish. She was up early and had breakfast ready for Jack Shefford when he came home the next morning. He looked tired but not as bad as she had really expected. She asked hopefully, 'Mum? Is she better?'

The man sat down by the table. 'No, she is still unconscious. I am going to ring the hospital during the day for any more news — and I shall go in again tonight.' He paused. 'Bertie, they say — if Mum comes through that she'll be ill a long time. I — don't know — how we'll manage.'

Jack had not meant that as a challenge, but Bertie worked automatically that day, with her father's words as a background to all she did. Her mother was going to be ill a long while. Then who was to look after the home and the twins? She knew it was a question she must answer before her father came home that evening.

When Jack returned to his mid-day meal there was no fresh news of his wife and when he had gone back to the shop Bertie went upstairs to see about fixing the curtains in the front bedroom. Only temporary ones had been put up and this morning those had fallen down. Standing on a chair to screw in a hook for the rod, she looked out towards the field opposite. Somewhere beyond was the common, hidden now by driving rain, and suddenly she remembered her thoughts as she went towards it for the first time not long ago – those pictures of herself at college . . . Ought she to give up her ambition to be a school-teacher — give it up and look after her family?

She had been so determined over what she was going to do with her life

. . . she and Elsie Marks together. They had been friends all through school — they had sworn to stick to one another always. They were going to the same college and then on to teach in the same school . . .

Her father came in to tea and he looked so tired that Bertie felt anxious. 'Dad, I've had my tea and the twins are in bed. You rest and let me go to the hospital.'

As he sat down at the table he glanced at the clock. 'No, no,' he replied. 'I *must* go.' She could not argue, but looking at his drawn face, she felt a sudden surge of affection. She glanced across at Dorothy who sat on a low stool near the fire, her head bent over a book. Then she said, 'I'll go upstairs to see your things are ready. You'll need to change — I can see your trouser-legs are wet.'

He was eating quickly and as she moved towards the door he said, 'It looks like clearing up now — and Dud Lambourne was in the shop just before

I closed. He is going to drive me into Scanlon.'

'Oh, I'm so glad you won't have to walk,' she answered.

Upstairs she put everything as nearly ready as she could for her father and then stood waiting for him.

She heard his quick step and looked up at him as he entered the bedroom. 'Dad,' she said, 'of course you know that as long as you need me I'll stay here. I'm not going back to school.'

She saw the relief which flashed into his eyes, but it was followed quickly by doubt. 'But Bertie . . . '

'There's no time to argue, Dad, and my mind really is made up. You must get ready now — but I had to tell you.'

'You don't seem to mind too much . . . ' He still sounded uncertain and she looked back at him as she began to close the door. 'I'm going to love looking after you,' she told him brightly. But as she went down the stairs her face was puckered. Dad must not know about the battle she had waged all day.

Yet that night she was glad she had made her decision. It was late when her father returned from the hospital. And one glance at his face told her before he spoke that Mum would never be coming back.

★ ★ ★

It was amazing how quickly the household began to revolve round Bertie as naturally as it had round her mother. At first she thought she would never get used to life without the older woman and often wondered how Mrs. Shefford had coped so efficiently. To Bertie it was hard going. She had never liked house-work, yet now she had to do it and was determined to do her best.

Dorothy started school and Bertie missed her help with the twins. She always knew that with the dependable Dorothy around the two younger ones would not get into mischief.

During those cold January days her father's face held a withdrawn expression that hid the grief he was feeling, and Bertie felt helpless to give any comfort.

Bertie saw quite a bit of Mr. Fawley who spent a lot of time in his garden and was always friendly. One day he called to her and said, 'Do you remember I told you my niece was coming?'

Bertie nodded.

'Well, she arrives today. Shall I bring her in to meet you?'

'Yes, yes . . . Does she like children? Has she any brothers and sisters of her own?' Bertie asked.

'She is the only girl. She has brothers but she is the youngest.' He paused. 'We haven't seen Marcia since she was about ten — and she was rather spoilt then. Mrs. Fawley is picturing her as a made-up doll and . . . ' He put up his hand to rub the side of his face, a habit he had when worried, and Bertie said comfortingly, 'Oh, all modern girls aren't like that. I expect you'll find she's jolly enough when she gets here.'

'I don't know.' Mr. Fawley wasn't easily consoled. 'I only wish she'd be like you, Bertie.'

'Not many girls are tomboys like me!' she laughed. 'If she wants to come and see you she will surely make it her business to please you.'

'But that's the trouble. Marcia has been ill, and it is my sister sending her . . . '

Bertie picked the sage she had gone out to fetch and as she went indoors she felt some qualms herself about the newcomer. Mr. Fawley obviously expected her to entertain the visitor but *if* she was as he imagined, then Bertie was not going to enjoy the experience.

They were just finishing their tea when the knock sounded on the door. 'Oh dear!' Bertie jumped up quickly, very conscious of the muddled tea table. Nesta had upset custard and

David a cup of tea. She wondered if she could hurriedly sweep it all away to the kitchen but the knock came again and sinkingly sure that this was the looked-for Marcia, she went to answer the door.

Outside was Mr. Fawley and with him an unknown girl. 'Come in,' Bertie invited, well aware of the lack of cordiality in her voice, and led the way into the living-room. A hasty thought had come to take them into the front room but it was so cold today, and Mr. Fawley would have considered her unfriendly.

'Would you like a cup of tea?' she asked and though she was not looking at Marcia, was certain that the other girl's glance had swept the tea-table before she said in a slow husky tone, 'Oh, no thank you.'

'Well, sit down, will you? And you children come and be introduced,' Bertie ordered.

'But we are interrupting their tea,' Mr. Fawley demurred.

'Oh no, they have finished,' she assured him.

The children regarded Marcia solemnly and silently, refusing to say more than 'Hullo,' and Bertie found the visit rather heavy going. And all the time she was wondering whether she could ever find any common ground with this girl, who was dressed so smartly. Marcia certainly wore make-up, but it was clever, accentuating her china-doll appearance, while her hands made Bertie want to hide her own, which were so unlike those slender white ones, with long tapering fingers and pointed, scarlet nails. Surely no one with nails like that could do any work.

Marcia sat comfortably in the old armchair that Jack always used, her slim legs crossed, displaying fine nylon stockings that were only distantly related to the sensible ones Bertie took for granted as necessary to cover her own stocky ankles and calves.

Bertie herself perched on the edge of a chair, one arm round each of the twins. Conversation lagged and Marcia made no attempt to keep it going and at last Bertie said, 'I don't know how you will like Cordery. I expect you are used to the town and may miss the life of it.'

'Oh well! I suppose I'll survive. It is only for a short while. The doctor was insistent I must rest and have fresh air — I imagine I can get big doses of that here.'

She gave a little grimace. 'I can always take a book to bed when I'm fed-up.' The girl's voice was so studiedly bored that Bertie felt a surge of indignation. After all, Mr. and Mrs. Fawley had to put up with her. She felt she would like to tell Marcia that in being bored she was likely to bore her uncle and aunt as well.

'I'm hoping you girls will be great friends, anyway.' Mr. Fawley's brow was puckered as he glanced from one to the other. 'You will find the time occasionally to take Marcia out?' he suggested, and his glance was so appealing that

Bertie's tone was hearty for his sake.

'Oh yes! I usually manage to get out every day. I go most often for a walk with Joe — that's our wee dog. He's a dear. Do you like dogs?' She was looking at Marcia who gave a shrug. 'Some of them,' she said.

Bertie laughed. 'Well, if you come across the common you are sure to meet a type you like. Ours is small — but you should see Bill Newbury's!'

'Bill Newbury . . . ' Marcia repeated the name slowly. 'Who is he — a friend of yours?'

Bertie's smile vanished and suddenly she wished she had not mentioned Bill. She answered casually, 'Oh he just takes his dog over the common — the same as I take Joe. That's how we first got to know one another — Joe had a fight with Bill's Rusty.'

'I . . . see . . . ' Marcia stood up, and her yawn sent a fresh surge of annoyance through Bertie. 'I feel I'm starting out on a new phase of my education — seeing the way the country yokels take their dogs walking . . . '

Bertie shut the door and stood for a moment leaning against it. Nasty little *urban* weed . . . Would she ever be able to stand the girl — even for Mr. Fawley's sake?

'Bertie, can I have a bit more cake, please?' David's plaintive demand started her back towards the living-room. Marcia might be an urban weed, but she was a very lovely one . . . as beautiful as a daisy — all pink and white. But she hadn't got a daisy's modest nature . . .

To Bertie's surprise Marcia arrived the next afternoon. The other girl was wearing a fur coat with a little matching fur hat. She looked so soft and brown that she reminded Bertie of a furry caterpillar.

'Do take pity on me,' Marcia drawled, 'and come for a walk. I cannot stand another minute of Aunt Nellie's ailments.'

'It can't be much fun to be as poorly as your aunt is,' Bertie retorted. 'She can rarely get out.'

'It can't be funny for Uncle Frank, either, to have to live with her,' Marcia said. 'If you ask me, Aunt Nellie's ailments are a good deal in her imagination.'

'Well, Mr. Fawley never complains,' Bertie answered, a trifle hotly, 'so we won't talk about her either. It seems disloyal, somehow.' Marcia followed her into the living-room, and stood in front of the fire. She gave Bertie an amused glance.

'You're so different from any of the girls I've ever known. Uncle Frank says you're more like a boy — and I believe he's right! You'd never be catty, would you?'

Bertie laughed then.

'I hope not!' she retorted. 'Well, we'll have to take the twins and Joe, you know. I hope you won't mind the cavalcade.'

Oddly enough Marcia did not seem bored by their walk over the common. When they turned to go back she remarked, 'We haven't seen your boy-friend.'

'No.'

'You didn't tell me he was the doctor's son,' Marcia added.

'Didn't I?'

'That you did not. Is *he* going to be a doctor?'

'No.' Bertie did not want to talk to Marcia about Bill, but the other girl persisted, 'I thought doctors' sons always followed their father's profession.'

'Bill isn't going to. He's training to be a civil engineer.'

'Oh! To make bridges and things like that?'

'I suppose so.'

When they got back to the Fawley's gate Marcia asked, 'You'll be going out again tomorrow?'

Bertie hesitated, tempted to prevaricate. Saturday was the day when she almost invariably met Bill . . . But her innate honesty was too strong and she found herself saying, 'I take Joe tomorrow afternoon but the twins and Dorothy stay with Dad in the shop usually on Saturdays. He'll never be responsible for the nips alone, but if Dorothy is there to keep an eye on them he doesn't mind.'

So the next afternoon, with Joe racing madly ahead of them, the two girls started down the lane towards the common. Bertie kicked stones along, and with her hands thrust deep into her pockets, gazed straight ahead. It was the last day of January and, though the wind was cold, the sun was bright.

Had she been alone Bertie would have run as wildly as Joe, who kept looking round — as though begging for his usual romping playmate. Alone she would have looked eagerly for Bill. As it was, she kept wishing that he would not appear. Marcia had spoken disparagingly of 'country yokels' — not realising she was talking about the doctor's son. Bertie did not *want* Marcia and Bill to meet. Before she reached her usual point she turned to go back.

Perhaps they would miss Bill, she thought, and in almost the same instant heard a deep-throated bark, followed by several of Joe's staccato yaps. Rusty and Joe were the best pals now.

Somewhere not far away was Bill ... Bertie could not define her reluctance to see Bill and Marcia meet, but deep in her heart she had a sense of foreboding.

And then Bill was there. He came over the rise, outlined against the sky — so big and with his easy grace of movement, his black untidy hair and dark eyes — so good to look at. That was what Bertie thought every time she saw him and now he came down the incline, swinging his stick and stopping as he reached them. Neither of the three spoke for a moment, but Bill's eyes were on Marcia and the admiration in them was undisguised.

Bertie said quickly, 'This is Marcia Fawley, Bill. She is staying next door to us for a while.'

'Not *too* little a while, I hope,' Bill

said, looking at Marcia. 'You are a sight worth seeing over our hum-drum common.'

'And you are, maybe, worth a visit to Cordery — from my point of view,' the girl drawled. Bertie scowled. The two of them meeting for the first time and handing out stupid meaningless flatteries . . .

She gave a little whistle to Joe and began to move away.

Bill had not seemed to see her before. Now he demanded, 'Hey, Bertie, where are you going?'

'Home,' she retorted. 'We are on our way back.'

'Oh no! You can't do that,' he told her.

'Oh yes I can.' Bertie moved another step away from him, and then added, 'Marcia can do what she likes. *I* am not a lady of leisure.'

Again she whistled to Joe, and then marched steadily off — head high, hands as usual thrust into her pockets. For the first time in her life she was rebelling against everything that went to make up Bertie Shefford. No wonder Bill had been unable to see *her* — set by the side of the utter femininity that was Marcia Fawley, with her fair curls clinging to the edge of her little fur hat, her perfect complexion, her even sparkling teeth . . .

Bertie kicked a stone viciously and Joe scampered after it, but she could not smile at his antics today. She was thinking — Me . . . I'm a good sort, with a brown face and teeth all uneven. Again a stone went flying. A good sort — that's what they think I am because I don't mind the wind and the weather. Because I'll listen when they want to talk. Because my name is Bertie and so I'm 'rather like a boy.' Suddenly her face crumpled. But I want to be liked. I want to be admired — like Marcia. Oh, Bill, can't you see how much I care for you? Bill, I want you to love *me*.

When she reached the general store Bertie greeted the girl behind the counter with, 'Hullo Lily.'

'Oh, you haven't been long today,' came the quick reply. 'Cold across the common?'

'No, there are several jobs I want to tackle at home,' Bertie answered, making her way towards the back room where she knew she would find the twins and Dorothy with their father.

Lily smiled, 'You won't be too popular — coming so soon. The kids have just begun on a game I've found when I was cleaning out cupboards. There isn't half a lot of old junk stored up here. It's about time a woman came along to have a go at this place.'

A woman! Bertie's lips twitched in a smile. Lily had only just left school, but she looked a lot younger than her fifteen years. A round baby face was set on a thin neck. The rest of her seemed to be mostly arms and legs. And using the word 'kids' so nonchalantly. Why, Dorothy with her serious eyes, could be years older than this half-grown girl.

In the back room the children were sitting on the floor round a highly coloured board. David was twisting a handle which stood in the middle of it. All three of them looked up at their sister. 'Oh no! We aren't going home . . . not yet we aren't.'

Bertie felt a sudden unwarranted rush of irritation against Lily — who was direct cause for this rebellion by providing the game. Then immediately she felt contrition. The fault was really her own. She had come back early because . . .

But she wouldn't let herself remember Bill, still out on the common with Marcia.

That evening when Jack Shefford came indoors he gave a little chuckle which had been familiar to Bertie as long as she could recall. Almost it had seemed part of him so that, since her mother's death, he had been someone different — a sober-faced man who never smiled. Now all at once he was again the Dad she knew.

He said, 'Lily is such a quaint little piece. She comes out with the queerest sayings at times. Just after we closed tonight she announced that from now on we are to have a New Rule. When I enquired what it was she said we will clear up the shop each evening and change the calendar to next day's date. Well, I'll admit it is often a bit of a rush in the mornings so in future we 'organise overnight' as she puts it.'

Bertie smiled too. 'Don't forget you are the boss, though,' she warned, her eyes twinkling. 'You must not let your customers see that slip of a thing ordering you around!'

Jack moved towards the table and his daughter saw that his face had settled back into the sombre lines which had become lately so familiar to her. Following him she put a hand on his arm. 'Dad, are you still worried about — money? Perhaps I could get some sort of a job to help out.'

'No, no.' He swung round to face her. 'You have job enough here,' he protested. 'Oh, I know I left a pretty bad debt behind me . . .'

'But it wasn't your fault.'

'Not entirely,' he answered. 'I suppose I was unlucky. But it is my duty to pay off every penny I owe. And I'll do it. Bertie, it will mean that we are not very flush for perhaps several years.'

'I don't mind that,' she put in quickly. 'Only I don't like to see you looking so unhappy and worried.'

He patted her hand. 'Then I'll try to be happier — for your sake,' he promised.

3

The days of that spring were like a heap of pearls to Bertie — every one of different quality, yet each holding something of beauty and delight. She, who had dreaded the irksomeness of household tasks, was finding herself thrilled by the garden. Time after time she would pause for a moment to look out of the window or even go outside the door.

The first thing to attract her was the grassy bank which surrounded their plot. One day she suddenly noticed among the grass a host of tiny green spears, and when her father arrived home at mid-day she pounced on him. 'Come and look,' she commanded. 'I believe we are going to have a lot of flowers here. No, don't tell me if you know what kind they are. Let me see them grow and find out.'

Jack Shefford smiled down into her glowing face. 'Although you were brought up in the town, you have inherited my love of the country,' he told her.

'I don't know whether I have inherited it,' she laughed, 'but I am in love with Cordery already. The common, the trees, the garden . . . I feel all excited down inside when I think of the year beginning and me to see all its first seasons here.'

'The common — you put that first,' Jack remarked as he followed her indoors.

'Did I?' But of course it had been natural to think most of the common — and she did not have to share it now with Marcia. The other girl's convalescence, originally supposed to be 'a week or a fortnight', had stretched to five weeks and during that time Bertie had not once seen Bill. But she felt it was more bearable that way, rather than having to watch him in Marcia's company. Now the other girl had left.

55

How Bertie watched the banks round the garden — but at last it was Dorothy who found the first bud, a tiny, baby daffodil. Before long their home was ringed by a fence of nodding yellow blooms. Bertie was so thrilled that every morning her first thought was to peep out at the golden host, and every night she would press her face against the cool glass to get a last glimpse of them in the moonlight.

One day, answering a knock at the door, she found a woman outside with a big empty basket. 'Are you selling the daffodils?'

'Selling the daffodils?' Bertie repeated, nonplussed.

'The last folk in this house always sold to me. All the cottages here sell the flowers, you know,' she added, seeing Bertie's incredulous expression.

Sell her banks of golden treasure? Of course she could not do that! But she could not keep them, it seemed, without a struggle. Every day she had requests to buy them.

Once, after four gypsy women had offered to take the the lot and named their price, Bertie felt a trifle guilty at turning away the money and confessed as much to her father. That would have gone a long way towards buying a coat for David.

'David shall have his coat,' Mr. Shefford promised. 'You keep your banks of gold. Especially this year, when you are getting so much pleasure from them, I'd hate to know you had sold them for gypsy cash.'

When Bertie realised that the daffodils were dying she looked at her father with wistful eyes. 'I want to keep them always,' she lamented.

'They are still there, waiting for next year,' he answered. 'Besides, come and look.'

On the ground, close beneath the banks, more flowers were growing. She stooped to peer at the small closely-packed green heads which she had not noticed before.

'They look like tiny corn cobs, Dad,'

she said. 'Oh, a garden is exciting.'

Jack's delight was as great as his daughter's for he was rediscovering what she was meeting for the first time. 'Your cobs won't be yellow,' he told her. 'They'll be blue.'

So Bertie's regret at the passing of the daffodils was lessened as she watched the making of a glorious carpet of bluebells, followed soon by the appearance of some enormous foxgloves. The children had not entirely shared their sister's enthusiasm over the other flowers, because they had been forbidden to pick them — but the foxgloves were a never-failing source of delight. Continually, as the large bells dropped, they were pounced upon and fitted on small fingers to form 'gloves' sometimes all pink, sometimes white, quite often mixed.

And the twins loved the common just as much as Bertie did, for now that the weather was better she took them with her as well as Joe. They all found great enjoyment in the sandy tracks which meandered in different directions between the heathland and, with Bertie's help, all sorts of games were devised.

Once they met Dud and he was made to join in the fun. 'We wanted a wild animal to come along,' David cried. 'His coat's all shaggy and brown — he's a lion.'

The man never said much but he always seemed perfectly at ease with the children. Now he gave a most realistic roar and the twins scuttled away to find hiding-places behind low bushes. 'Come on, Bertie,' they called. 'You'll get eaten!' She gave a laugh and then she, too, ran for cover.

'You are expected now to stalk us,' she called gaily to Dud, but suddenly his attitude had altered. He shook his head and began to hurry away, while at the same moment Bertie heard a familiar bark. Rusty!

David and Nesta were raising cautious heads and all at once David shouted, 'The lion's gone but here's . . . here's . . . '

'An elephant,' Nesta supplied. 'Must be — he's grey.'

Bertie stood up, suddenly aware of her dishevelled appearance. It hadn't mattered about Dud, but Bill had the power to make her heart beat wildly and wish desperately that she could look a little more like Marcia Fawley.

Bill strode along and suddenly the twins were upon him. 'You're a 'lephant,' David said, while Nesta gave him a shove. 'It's elephant,' she announced. 'Come on, make a noise like one and chase us.'

Bill gave Bertie a sympathetic glance.

'Can't kids be a nuisance sometimes! You must be a hero to put up with them,' he told her, but all at once the girl's eyes flashed the signs of battle.

'Goodness!' she exclaimed. 'I'm not so old that I can't play with them myself! Would you have thought you were a nuisance when you were David's age?'

He looked at her with amusement. 'I most probably was!' he laughed, and with a sudden movement put out his hand to give her cheek a small pinch. 'You look so red and indignant. I think I shall call you Bertie the Defender. That funny little tyke of Dud's, Dud himself, and now the kids — with the least provocation you fly to their defence. But I like to see your feathers rise.' He chuckled teasingly, and Bertie turned away feeling *covered* in feathers which were distinctly ruffled.

Yet she couldn't help loving this big broad-shouldered young man. She glanced back before she began to descend the knoll. The twins and Joe were on ahead. She heard David call that another game was starting and ordering her to hurry, but she paused long enough to see that Bill was going down towards the stream and to remember how he had said before Marcia's advent, 'You wait till the spring comes — then I'll have something to show you in the brook that will amuse you.'

Perhaps he had forgotten. Perhaps

he just did not want to bother with her.

But one day at the end of March she met him, and she was alone except for Joe. 'Hullo,' he said and turned, walking back with her towards the stream. As they reached a small plank bridge he pointed down into the clear water. 'Look,' he ordered, 'and start counting!' She peered down into the brook and then glanced up at Bill.

'It's hundreds and hundreds of tiny fish,' she exclaimed. 'Oh, I must bring the nips to show them these.'

'Minnows,' Bill told her. 'Better let them bring some pins and cotton to catch them.'

'Catch them?' Her tone was incredulous. 'You never could.'

'Yes you could,' he laughed, 'but a jam jar on a string is the best way.'

She was fascinated and he watched her with a smile in his eyes. 'You're a funny little thing, Bertie,' he said at last. 'You get so enthusiastic over the things that seem so ordinary to me — a little stream and minnows, for instance.'

The girl got up quickly. From his tone he might have been speaking to a child — and she hated him to think of her like that. She said slowly, 'But you haven't lived in a town all your life. I have, you know.'

'No.' He began to move away along the narrow path and, looking back at her, grinned, 'I can tell you this — it's not *many* town folk who go crazy about the country.'

She did not answer. He hadn't mentioned one particular town girl, but he was thinking of her. *Marcia* was sophisticated and hated the common when it was wet or very windy. Marcia, with her delicate doll looks and her assumed ennui — she was the sort of girl he liked . . .

'Aren't you coming? Joe and Rusty are miles ahead.' His voice broke into her thoughts and she began to follow him.

A moment or two later he pointed across the heath as he said, 'Look, there's Dud Lambourne. He's excavating again, I suppose. He must be soft to imagine he'll ever find anything among that heap of rubble he is always poking over.'

Bertie felt the familiar thrill of indignation at a jibe against Dud. No one who was 'soft' could work White Farm as he did. But suddenly she remembered Bill's sardonic voice when he said, 'Bertie the Defender,' and she bit back the words which had leapt to her lips. Instead she asked, 'What is that heap of stones over there?'

'That's Cordery Abbey,' Bill replied. 'Monks were supposed to have come from France and started it centuries ago.'

'But — that little heap of stones an Abbey!' she exclaimed, and the man laughed.

'You talk to Dud about it,' he told her. 'He could tell you its history — that is if he can find his tongue to talk to you. He opens his mouth like a cod at me but never says anything.'

Bertie looked round at him and now her eyes were blazing. 'You can be unkind,' she said. Then abruptly she stooped and, picking up a stone, threw it for Joe to chase after. She didn't want Bill to laugh at her again. Bill's teasing had power to hurt. Yet she felt a trifle guilty that she had not been more voluble in Dud's defence. It was unfair of Bill to make fun of the other young man.

As she neared home a little later she overtook Mr. Fawley and slowed to walk beside him. He smiled at her and said, 'I've news for you. Marcia has a job in Scanlon, so I expect we'll be seeing a bit of her. Mrs. Fawley is glad, though, that she will not be actually living with us.'

'Oh!' There seemed no other answer to this surprising news and after a pause Mr. Fawley added, 'I'm thinking that perhaps young Newbury is the attraction.'

'I don't know.' They reached his gate and she escaped. She *did* know. Of course Bill was the magnet.

Marcia was back and the common would again lose some of its attraction for Bertie. In fact even now she felt she wanted to avoid Bill. He probably knew that Marcia was coming to Scanlon. He might want to talk about her — Bertie did not.

She crammed her days as full of work as possible, and soon she found that she was able to accept the other girl's return — if not gladly, at least with equanimity. And nothing was able to dim her pleasure in the garden.

At the bottom of it there were all sorts of fruit trees and, remembering how forlorn their patch had looked in January, Bertie was thrilled by the magic of the trees' awakening. It was in April that she first became aware that Prince Spring was making his advances. His initial conquest was Princess Pear. Shyly she opened a hundred little green eyes all over her recently bare boughs. Then in just a day or two, it seemed, she was decked in a beautiful white wedding gown. Prince Spring was certainly a hasty wooer . . .

But like King Solomon he wanted many wives. In quick succession Duchess Cherry and Marchioness Apple fell victims to his caresses — and Bertie was not sure which bridal finery she liked best for each was vying for supremacy.

The apple, with her tiny pink posies surrounded by a wreath of green, was very lovely. But wait, in Mr. Fawley's garden there were other brides. Bertie held her breath in delight that morning when she went out and really saw the huge laburnum for the first time. Cascades of golden flowers — oh, she couldn't describe it. By her own side wicket there was a tiny laburnum with about a couple of strings of bloom — could that ever be like this thing of golden glory? Nothing could be more beautiful than this — a decision she was to modify a day or two later when another tree near the road was arrayed in a mass of white and pink blossoms.

Mr. Fawley told her it was a Japanese cherry — its only job being to delight folk in springtime, she thought one day as she went up the road. If only she could keep this parade of beauty all the year round. She had never realised the wonder of Springtime before.

But indoors Bertie did not find things so enchanting. Her cookery often turned out a failure, and she dropped things. 'I'm sure I was never meant to be a housewife,' she told herself ruefully one day as she stood looking down in dismay at the apple pie she had dropped on the floor. At least this time the dish was not broken but she'd have to hurry to get anything else done in time for dinner.

Sometimes she half-expected her father to get cross with her — they could so ill afford breakages and waste — but Jack Shefford was always patient.

There was another day when she was doing some washing in the kitchen, having left the twins playing happily with their bricks. Suddenly Nesta rushed out of the living-room. 'David's lit a fire!' she cried excitedly.

'Lit a fire?' Bertie repeated, hastily drying her hands and following the small girl. David was squatting on the floor, his round face absorbed as he looked at his handiwork. Behind Jack's armchair he had built a fireplace with his wooden bricks. Dominoes were obviously meant to be coal, under which paper was already burning, helped by another piece which he was using as a fan.

'David!' Bertie rushed across the room. Flames were beginning to reach upwards to the curtains hanging beside a french door. She grabbed for a cushion from the chair and threw it down on the miniature fire, pressing it firmly with her hands till all the flames were extinguished.

'David, you *are* naughty.'

Bertie surveyed the scorched lino and bricks, the smoke mark which showed right up the back of her father's chair.

'You might have had the whole house

alight,' she told her small brother, and knew that somehow she ought to punish him.

There was a knock on the back door and she heard Joe rush along the passage, giving a series of little barks — not the noise he made when the coalman or some gypsies knocked. *Then* he made a dreadful fuss, trying to make it sound as though he was as big as Rusty.

She went quickly to the door — to find Dud outside. He waved his arm towards the lane, and she saw his little van was by the gate. 'Th . . . thought the n . . . nips might like a ride up the d . . . drove,' he suggested and added he was going to a farm where some new puppies had recently been born.

'How nice of you to think of coming in,' she said. 'They'd love it . . . ' Then she paused. 'But I simply can't let them go now. I can't let them have a *treat* after what has just happened.' She told him about the fire and he smiled his slow smile, saying it might not be fair to punish Nesta.

'No? But I have an idea she was really the instigator,' Bertie replied. 'She usually is.'

The young man began to turn away and she put out a quick hand to touch his sleeve. 'Dud, you are not minding? You'll come again another day when I could let them go?' He nodded, his brown eyes gently understanding.

Nesta and David came slowly to the door — in time to see Dud getting into his van. He saw them and waved, and they would have run out into the garden but with a restraining hand on each small shoulder, Bertie said, 'Dud came to take you for a ride to see some puppies — and you would have gone but for your naughtiness.'

She saw David's lip quiver and felt that perhaps she was being cruel. She hated to give punishments — her own childhood was close enough for her to remember how it felt to be deprived of a treat. But she steeled her heart. She said, 'Go and clear up those bricks, both of you.'

And she hoped very much that Dud would come another day — before those puppies were too big.

It was on a Saturday when he came next and she was standing looking at a huge lupin bush by the gate. He got out of his van and came towards her. 'Dud, this has been worth waiting for,' she exclaimed. 'I have been longing for it to come out but I have dared Mr. Fawley to tell me what colour it would be. And how it smells. People passing the gate remark on the sudden lovely whiff of scent it gives them.'

'Um . . . It smells like honey,' Dudley returned. He talked to Bertie now, slowly, but with scarcely the trace of a stammer.

'That's why the bees love it — they can smell the honey,' he said.

Bertie shook her head vigorously. 'It smells like lupin — and nothing else,' she declared, laughing.

'You are always so emphatic,' he

replied, while his rare smile lit his eyes to dancing brightness. 'It's the *colour* of your hair.'

The girl looked at him in surprise. 'Dud!' she exclaimed. Then she laughed lightly. 'I can deny that too,' she told him. 'My straw is not a tiny bit like this beautiful lupin, which is . . . oh, a deep, deep cream . . . '

As she paused Dud said he had come hoping she would let the children go with him today. 'Dorothy and Joe too,' he ended.

'Oh, that would help me,' she answered. 'I want to go into Scanlon to see if I can get a tortoise for Dorothy's birthday — another girl has one and only a tortoise will satisfy Dorothy.' She heard the church clock strike and said, 'If I hurry I'll get the next bus.'

Not long afterwards she was walking briskly under the tall pines which lined the road. As she neared the bus stop she was thinking of what Dud had said to her. 'I'll have to tell Dad that I am being paid compliments now!' she told herself, smiling.

Then suddenly her merriment died, leaving only an odd feeling of warmth. 'No I won't tell even Dad,' she decided. 'He would think it was funny, and it *is* unkind to laugh at poor old Dud.'

She looked up at the blue sky, unevenly edged by the tops of the trees on either side of her. It was a lovely day, yet Bertie was not as happy as she ought to be. Deep in her heart was the now acknowledged longing to see Bill Newbury again. Just to see him . . .

When she had made her purchase she started homewards. There was no bus going to Cordery for ages so she had to walk. She was turning into the road leading to the village when she heard a hail and on the other side of the road saw that a motor cycle had been stopped.

'Bill!' she exclaimed, crossing towards him, and then gazing at the shining machine on which he sat astride. 'Is it yours?'

He nodded, grinning in delight at her

surprise. 'How do you like her?' he demanded. 'I only bought her today.' He waved a hand in the direction of the pillion seat. 'Going to let me give you a lift?'

'Oh Bill! That would be lovely.' Her grey eyes sparkled. 'But not too fast, mind. I have a precious cargo.'

'Oh — what?'

She told him about Dorothy's birthday wish and laughed. 'There were dozens of tortoises in the pet shop and when I'd chosen one I hadn't anything to put it in. I believe the man thought I was a bit mad.'

'Maybe he thought you had the idea you could lead it home on a string,' Bill teased.

'Anyway, I didn't try. I bought a paper carrier. Look — it's such an odd little thing. I'm sure it's frightened already. You won't shake it up too much, will you?'

'It will survive, don't you worry. Come on — hop up.'

It seemed only moments before they

were stopping outside her gate and Bertie said, 'It was wonderful, Bill — thank you.'

He smiled down into her glowing face as he said, 'I hope the cargo is all right.' Then after a pause he asked, 'Have you seen Marcia lately? She's working in Scanlon now, you know.'

The brightness faded from Bertie's face. 'Mr. Fawley told me she was coming, but I didn't know she had arrived . . . '

A moment or two later with a roar of the engine he was gone up the road, and slowly Bertie went indoors. Marcia was in Scanlon and Bill had a motorbike — it was impossible not to know the two facts were connected.

She put the tortoise down in a corner of the veranda. Now it was just an oval lump of shell. Poor wee thing — it *had* got shaken up rather too well. She only hoped it would wake up before Dorothy got home.

When the children arrived back they were eager to tell of their outing. 'Can't we have one of the puppies?' they asked.

'Oh no!' she exclaimed. 'We already have Joe.'

She said nothing about the new arrival until tea was over. Then she took Dorothy outside the french door and pointed to the corner. The little girl ran across the veranda and, stooping down, said, 'Oh, my Timmy!'

'Why Timmy?' Bertie asked.

'It's a nice name,' Dorothy retorted and then, bending over, asked, 'Hasn't it got any head?'

'Yes — I think it is asleep.'

David and Nesta arrived too and the three children squatted on their heels, patiently watching. It was just when a visitor appeared that a little black nose was cautiously peeping out and drawing back. Bertie heard the footsteps coming along the path from the side wicket before she saw the girl. Then she came round the corner of the house.

'Hullo, Marcia.' Bertie tried to sound cordial.

'Mr. Fawley told me you were coming to Scanlon to work,' she said, and despised herself that she had not mentioned Bill as giving the latest news. 'Won't you sit down?' she invited.

Marcia took a deck chair and Bertie flopped down on the lawn, studying the other girl through narrowed lids. Bertie had almost forgotten how really flawless was her complexion, how very soft and curling was her hair . . .

Bertie ground a heel into the grass. Straw for hair . . . uneven teeth . . . face that browned like a gypsy's and was dusted with freckles as soon as there was much sun . . . How crazy for anyone like that to love Bill Newbury.

Marcia was talking and suddenly she exclaimed, 'I don't believe you have heard a word I'm saying. I'm trying to tell you about Aunt Nellie. She is in a proper fume in there. I've promised Uncle Frank I'll ask you to go in and see her.'

'What is the matter with her?' Bertie asked. 'Come to think of it, I haven't seen Mr. Fawley today.'

'He daren't go in the garden, even, while there is a chance she may be dying!' Marcia said. 'But it's only one of her usual attacks of sciatica.'

Bertie got to her feet and Marcia stood up as well. 'I must go too,' she said.

The girl on the lawn watched her moving away — so trim and neat in her slim-fitting orange suit — going off to meet Bill of course.

Bertie turned with a quick, impatient gesture. She was recalling something Mrs. Fawley had once said to her, 'Marcia was made for ornament, not for use.'

But Bertie Shefford was strictly utilitarian — so it was not the niece who would help out in an emergency, but the little next-door neighbour.

4

It was in August that the glory Bertie had longed to see came to the common. She had known the heather was coming out but one day it seemed to be all of a sudden in full bloom. She stood on top of the knoll and looked out across a purple sea. It had been hot but now it was cooler — a perfect, windless evening. She caught the sound of bells — far-away but distinct on the still air. Out of the heather below her a small shape rose, spiralling higher and higher before starting its evening hymn.

Bertie thought, 'I want to hold this moment in my memory for ever. The heather, the bells, the skylark's song . . .'

Then the spell was broken by a deep-throated bark and Rusty came bounding towards her. He reached an eager, welcoming tongue for her face and she laughed.

She knew that Bill must be some-where close but she could not see him. 'Where is your master?' she asked the dog which pranced round her. 'Go on — where's Bill?'

Rusty turned to leap ahead of her and she went on down the steep track behind him, coming after a moment or two into a deep, grassy depression that was completely hidden from the view of the path. Bill was lying on his back but he sat up as she appeared.

'So the nymph of the common invades my retreat,' he teased.

'Sometimes, Bill Newbury . . . ' She broke off and he patted the grass at his side. 'Come on, sit down — and then shoot. What name were you going to call me? I could see in your eyes that it was nothing good.'

She took her place at his side and then shook her head. Why tell him that she thought him unkind to call her a nymph? She was plain Bertie Shefford and he knew it. Coming from him 'nymph' was teasing — but it hurt.

'It's too perfect an evening for a quarrel,' she grinned at him.

They were silent for quite a long time until Bill said, 'What is the matter, Bertie? You are so quiet, when I expected you to start enthusing because the heather is out.'

She did not answer at once. Then she said seriously, 'You would probably laugh at me if I tried to tell you what I am feeling — and this evening is too precious . . . '

He gave her arm a sudden little pat. 'Have I given you the impression that I am so flippant?' he asked. 'Why do you think I am here now — don't you think *I* love the common when the heather is out?' Bending a little nearer to her, he said, 'Listen,' and pointed to the purple sweep on the hillock above them.

'Yes,' she told him, 'I have heard it ever since I sat down — yet I can't describe it . . . Not a drone or a buzz, but a continual murmur, like the muted sound of a comb played through paper.'

He gave her a quick glance before he said, 'Lean back a bit and squint across the heather with your eyes half-closed. You can imagine it is a mauve-coloured sea, moving gently.' When she had obeyed him he asked. 'See what I mean?'

She nodded. 'It's bees, isn't it?' She laid right back then and Bill followed her example. She knew that by putting out her hand she could touch him. Just she and Bill — alone in a world of bees and heather . . .

It was Bill who at last broke the spell by demanding, 'Where is Joe?'

'He wasn't very energetic. I don't know if he is unwell or whether it is just the hot weather.' Mundane reality had come into her hour with the mention of Joe. She sat up and after a moment scrambled to her feet.

'I'll have to go back,' she said. 'They were all in the garden, so I took french leave, but I won't stop long or they'll miss me and wonder where I am.'

'They'd probably guess — and know

you were safe with the doctor's son,' he answered, smiling as he stood up. She glanced at him and then away. Oh, she was glad she had come. This was a memory to store away that belonged to her and Bill alone. Slowly she turned to go, but Bill still lingered. He said quietly, ''Comin' through the crags o' Kyle, Amang the bonnie, blooming heather, There I met a bonnie lassie . . . She charmed my heart and aye sinsye I couldna think on any ither; By sea and sky she shall be mine! My bonnie lass amang the heather . . . ''

Bertie's heart was beating fast — wayward heart that could let her forget a moment that she was Bertie Shefford — plain and boyish-looking. She had let her hair grow but it did not make much difference.

But now her eyes were shining as she gazed up at Bill. 'Robbie Burns?' she asked. 'To think that you can quote him like that!' She waited. There was an odd expression in Bill's eyes.

'I quoted that to Marcia last night,'

he said. 'I believe she thought I was rather affected to spout poetry at her. But often it's easier to find someone else's words to fit our feelings . . . '

A pain that was almost physical was gripping Bertie's heart. She had thought this hour was *hers* — but Marcia was here. 'By the sea and sky she shall be mine.' The intense desire in Bill's tone had been for Marcia — and how, for those moments, could Bertie have been foolish enough not to know?

Bill and Marcia probably saw a lot of one another now — for Bill was training with a firm in Scanlon. Bill was Marcia's for the taking — yet she could be supercilious when he quoted Burns at her!

Before this evening Bertie could never have imagined Bill doing it, but 'love can make fools and angels of us all.' Who had said that?

Bertie leapt the first clump or two of heather and reached the path quickly. Bill followed. 'Here,' he called. 'You can't hurry on such a hot night as this.'

His long strides carried him towards her and she resisted the impulse to take to her heels and run away from him.

His eyes were full of the teasing light she knew so well. 'By the way, Bertie, you are almost as bad as Marcia — my quotation was not Burns but an old Scottish song . . . '

She felt a surge of anger against him. He had spoilt her perfect evening. She said, '*You* may not have to hurry, but *I* have,' and rushed away from him.

In her sudden wrath she told herself she did not want to see Bill ever again but only about three days later she met him — with the familiar quickening of her heart-beats, knowing a gladness that she would speak to him, hear his deep, teasing voice.

He came to meet her. He said, 'I'm sorry I upset the apple cart so badly the other night — I was picking up crab-apples all the way home!'

She could forgive him now. She said, 'Hope you didn't try eating them, then.'

'I have a peace-offering for you,' he

said, putting his hand in his pocket and then offering her two small pieces of pink paper.

'Tickets for 'No Bouquets for Lulu.' I have read one or two reviews about it.'

'Have you? So you know it's the latest of Kingsclere's musicals — pre-West-end presentation. A kind of dress-rehearsal, I suppose . . . '

Bertie glanced down at the tickets again and then back to Bill who was asking, 'Well, would you like to go?'

She nodded.

'That's all right then — if you can get away from those 'nips' of yours. The bus goes from the corner of Meek Road. Be there for the seven o'clock one on Friday evening — and be there early if you can so as to bag the front seat of the bus on top. I expect I'll make it by the skin of my teeth. You keep my seat.'

Bertie lived through the days between riding on the crest of a wave of happiness. She was going out with Bill — unbelievable almost. She had to keep telling herself it was true.

After a rush to get everything done on Friday, she left her gate and began to hurry along, but as she reached the house on the other corner she nearly bumped into Mr. Fawley, who was coming out.

'Why you *are* smart,' the man smiled, and she laughed gaily.

'It's not often you see me dressed up,' she said. 'I'm going to the theatre.'

'You deserve an outing, my dear. Now Marcia, who never seems to do anything to deserve it, is always going out — though just at the moment she has struck a bad patch. After getting this job at Scanlon she has had to go back home because her mother is ill. I'd like to go and see my sister too, but I can't very well leave Mrs. Fawley.'

He was walking at his usual slow pace beside her.

'No, I suppose not. I'm sorry about it,' Bertie said, and wondered how she could escape without seeming rude. She hadn't many minutes to reach the corner before seven o'clock . . .

But the man was saying, 'You run on, my dear — and enjoy yourself.'

'I expect I shall,' she replied. 'Goodbye.' She was rather breathless when she reached the bus stop, but relieved to find there were not many other folk waiting. She had time to think now and Mr. Fawley's news came back to her with a revealing knowledge that dimmed her happiness. Marcia had left Scanlon. Bill had bought those tickets, meaning to take the other girl tonight . . .

The bus rounded the corner and stopped. Bertie scrambled aboard and up the stairs, putting her handbag on the seat nearest the window. Bill was not here but she was obeying instructions. She might have known — she should have guessed there was some catch in it, for him to be taking *her*. Talking about peace-offerings — and her drinking it in!

Then she saw that the driver was preparing to get back in his cab, and almost in the same instant there came the sound of footsteps on the bus stairs.

She glanced round. Bill had come and she could not keep the welcome from her eyes. Bother Marcia — this was Bertie's own evening and she was going to enjoy every minute of it . . .

'Shove over,' Bill ordered. 'You can have the window seat.' He smiled at her. 'I only just made it. What would you have done if I *hadn't* turned up?'

'Gone on, of course. I should have been sure you would meet me the other end on your motor-cycle. By the way, why didn't you take me on it tonight?'

'Two reasons,' he answered. 'Most important I hadn't a crash helmet for you.'

The bus was starting and leaning forward she said, 'This is steep! Do you know, I've never been to Flinton.'

'I was hoping you hadn't,' he returned. 'You are such a satisfying person to show something to . . . and that was the other reason I didn't want to use the bike. You wouldn't have seen so well from the back of that.' He gestured at the slope below them. 'This is what we call the ups-and-downs. But you wait a bit.'

Above them on the right was a high, white cliff with flaming gorse and purple heather at its foot. On the left were fields beyond which a small hillock rose, green-clad, to more purple heather.

Bertie's eyes shone as they garnered each detail into the storehouse of her memory, ready to be brought out later for her father's ears.

Down into a valley they dipped, where a farmhouse stood beside a stream. She caught a glimpse of brown cows in fields to her right, while on the other side of the road sedgy bushes proclaimed boggy ground. With a grinding of gears they started up out of the dip, past a sprawling pottery works to a house perched in solitary state right on top of the hill. 'My, I expect they feel the wind up here,' she exclaimed, looking round at Bill for the first time.

'Now, don't miss this,' he told her, and pointed to what lay ahead of them. 'What do you think of that for hills?' he asked.

She caught her breath. Down and then up again — almost as steep as the walls of a house they looked from this vantage point, and involuntarily she caught Bill's arm as they started downwards to where a light-railway track ran across the road. Bump . . . bump . . . bump they went over the rails before they began on another grind upwards.

'How the nips would love this bumpity ride,' she laughed. 'I must bring them.' She glanced back at the stolid faces of several passengers behind them.

'I suppose the people here get used to your ups-and-downs, but I'm sure I never will.'

As they reached the top she asked, 'Is that the end of the hills?'

'No — another down and up,' he told her, 'but not as steep as the middle one. I thought you'd reckon that a corker.'

'What are the railway lines for?' she asked, glancing back. 'Surely they are never used.'

'Oh yes! There is a gravel pit back there on the left and a little engine chugs out occasionally, pulling a load of gravel, and fussily whistling at the top of its voice. There are more lines on the top of this hill too.'

'I had no idea there was anything so exciting to see this way. I must bring the twins to see the engine.' The man gave a little grin. 'You and your nips,' he said in a dry tone.

★   ★   ★

On the way home it was dark and as the bus began its jolting journey Bertie was silent. The tunes from the show were dancing gaily through her head. Bill was at her side. She felt quietly happy.

They were grinding up the last hill

when he asked, 'Well — enjoy it?'

'It has been grand. Bill, thank you for bringing me.'

They got out of the bus and the man took hold of her hand. 'It's pretty dark tonight,' he remarked.

'Yes, I don't mind, though,' she replied.

'I thought I would never get used to the dark roads after the town, but I like it here now . . .'

As they reached Bill's gate she slowed but, still holding her hand, he went past it. 'You don't really imagine I'd let you go home alone?' he asked. 'It *is* rather late, you know.'

Bertie had been out as late as this before — without an escort. But she did not put her thought into words and they walked on together.

Bill started to whistle and Bertie joined him. As they came to the end of the tune Bill said, 'Gosh — and you can whistle, can't you?'

She laughed. 'There's an old saying I have had quoted at me a good many times — A whistling woman and a crowing hen are never no good to God nor men. So now you know! But seriously, Bill, it was a lovely show. I believe I must be a middlebrow. I just can't appreciate heavy classics, and yet I don't like jazz — but when it comes to something like 'No Bouquets for Lulu' — well, I could go to that a dozen times and still want to go again.'

'Greedy-sides,' he teased. 'Are you fishing?'

'Oh Bill, no!'

He squeezed her hand. 'Anyway, old pal, this won't be the last time. When something else good comes along I'll take you again.'

He released her hand as they reached her gate and she went quietly along the path and into the dark, silent house.

Old pal . . . Yet even if he thought of her only as that — for tonight she was content.

★　★　★

Even when she heard from Mr. Fawley the following week that Marcia was back, she hugged the memory of that night out with Bill, treasured his promise to take her again . . .

But she did not see him across the common for days.

5

It was on an evening about the middle of August that Bertie went down the lane to the common on her own. Jack Shefford had decided to have a bonfire and the twins would not miss the fun of that so whistling for Joe she had left all the family behind.

The little dog ran excitedly along and, catching some of his spirit she raced with him over the knoll and down the further side towards the stream. She glanced all round her and then said aloud, 'You and I, Joe — all alone in the world.'

She picked up a stone and sent it spinning along the path. Joe chased after it and, laughing, the girl followed at a run. When she reached the plank bridge over the stream she halted. The minnows were there, bringing a memory of herself and Bill standing on this spot . . .

She stood there a long while watching the ceaseless movement of the tiny fishes below her, heedless of Joe's restless sallies till he began to yap in delight.

Then, looking up, she realised that Bill had almost reached her. 'Hullo,' he greeted her. 'Counting them?'

She smiled. 'I've reached two million and one — you can carry on from there,' she told him. But he made no answering quip, and she sensed that he was not in his usual teasing mood. His broad shoulders were hunched and his hands pushed deep in his pockets. His expression was almost morose as he stood silently by her side, gazing down into the water.

He said at last, 'Bertie, I've fallen out with Marcia.' A wild thrill of delight ran over her. She was *glad*. But he was saying, a note of pleading in his tone, '*You* might do something. You and Marcia are friends. It was through you I met her.'

Bertie did not answer. How little Bill knew of her relationship with Marcia. She had not been to Cordery for weeks. Friends! Anyway, why should Bertie try to patch up a quarrel between her and Bill?

He was saying urgently, 'Say you will help me, Bertie. It means so much to me.' He put his hand on her arm. 'Come on, be a good sort.'

She felt a wild desire to laugh and cry at the same time. Why should everyone assume she was 'a good sort?' At the moment she felt anything but good about Marcia — and Bill's touch sent waves of emotion tingling through her.

She turned away from him. 'Bill, what *could* I do?' She asked brusquely.

'I . . . don't know,' he said slowly, following her along the narrow path away from the stream, 'but I can't live without Marcia.'

They were silent till they reached the knoll. Then he said, 'You think I'm a sentimental fool, don't you?'

'No Bill. I think Marcia is a fool not

to love you as much as you obviously love her.' Still she did not look at him. For one mad moment she had hoped that if Marcia was out of the running there might be a chance for herself. Now sane common sense had come to her rescue — while her own love for him was prompting, 'If you really care you would want his happiness — something *you* can never give him.'

She said at last, 'Bill, quite honestly I can't see that I can help you but if anything turns up or I think of a way — then I'll do my best.'

He picked up a stone and sent it hurtling far ahead for Joe to chase. His shoulders were pulled back and his eyes had a suddenly hopeful expression. 'You're a pal,' he said. 'I don't feel half so bad now.'

They walked together to the top of the lane. Then Bill went in through the side gateway of Turbary Grange and Bertie went on alone. It was when she had almost reached home that she met Dud Lambourne.

He asked, 'Have you ever been across the common to the sea?'

'No!' she exclaimed. 'I didn't know you could do that.'

He gave his lop-sided grin. 'Like to go?' he asked, and she nodded.

'I could bring the pony and we could give the children rides.' He spoke slowly but he managed with very little stumbling.

Bertie's eyes were shining as she looked up at him. 'Dud, we could have a lovely day,' she said.

'N . . . next Saturday, then, if it's fine?'

It was not till she was in bed that night that some words danced unbidden through Bertie's mind, 'By sea and sky she shall be mine.' They were words which she could not forget and they made her watch next day for Dud. No matter how much she might want to see him she would not go to the farm, with the risk of seeing Mrs. Lambourne. So she was glad to hear at last the sound of a pony's hooves trotting along the lane.

Quickly she ran along the garden path.

'Dud,' she called and he pulled his horse to a halt.

'I'd like to ask Bill and Marcia to come on Saturday,' she told him and his face, which had lit at sight of her, suddenly had that wooden look which most people saw always.

He said, 'Bill won't want to come over the common with a pony, three nippers and — me.'

Bertie knew how true that was and she said hastily, 'My idea was to ask Bill and Marcia separately to meet us there. I want it to be a surprise for them both. You see, they have fallen out and . . . and . . . '

The man looked down at her with an odd expression in his brown eyes. 'You want them to make it up, eh?' He shook the pony's reins. 'All right,' he said, but after he had disappeared round the corner Bertie still stood at the gate. She was remembering Dud's words — the surprise in his voice as he said, 'You want them to make it up . . . ' Did Dud guess at what she thought was her own secret — her love for Bill?

She knew she could contact Bill all right, but Marcia was not so easy. She could write to the other girl but felt that a personal invitation might be more effective. She asked Mr. Fawley if he had any idea when his niece might possibly be coming next, and he shook his head.

'As a matter of fact Marcia's visits rather depress Mrs. Fawley,' he said slowly. 'It irks my wife that our niece is not like you, my dear.'

Bertie laughed merrily. 'Perhaps it's a good job there aren't too many like me,' she told her neighbour. 'What a time the poor men would have — surrounded by plain-Jane Berties!'

Then Bertie found she had to go to Scanlon and she determined to find Marcia out. She managed to get to the other girl's office just before lunch-time and by luck met Marcia as she came from a passage at the side of the building where she worked.

'Oh, I'm glad I've met you, Marcia. I'm taking the children to Riley Chine on Saturday. Would you like to come along? Bertie saw the hesitation in the girl's eyes and felt irritated when she shrugged slim shoulders and said, 'Riley Chine with your kids? She paused and then added, 'Couldn't be more boring than Scanlon on a Saturday, though . . . Perhaps I'll come, especially if there is the chance of a swim . . . '

'I hadn't thought of swimming,' Bertie admitted, but if that formed an attraction to Marcia all to the good. She said, 'We'll expect you then.'

Marcia was already moving away and glancing back she returned, 'Don't count on me for sure.'

Bertie watched her go and thought, Not for sure because if anything less 'boring' turns up then Marcia won't want Riley Chine and my kids . . .

With a little impatient movement Bertie turned away. Bill's a fool, wanting her — but I'm more of a fool to be doing this. And that reflection became a real regret that she had launched the idea — especially when Saturday dawned clear and sunny — a perfect day which could be easily ruined by her attempt to be a peace-maker.

The journey over the common was great fun. Even Dorothy, usually reserved, took her turn at riding Dud's pony, and her glowing cheeks showed her excited happiness at the novel means of transport. Dud had decided to start early and go slowly — a plan which appealed to them all except Joe. He was constantly capering ahead, as though urging them to hurry up.

When they reached the heap of stones which Bill had said was the ruins of Cordery Abbey, Bertie pointed and asked, 'You often dig there, Dud. Do you think you might unearth something interesting?'

As he looked around at her his brown eyes were alight. 'I have found several things already,' he said in a low voice, 'but nothing important — only enough to show it is worth while going on.'

He was leading the pony with David astride and, halting, he said, 'We'll go over to the ruins and eat the apples I've brought.'

Bertie came at the rear of the small procession and glancing round curiously remarked, 'It looks like a heap of very ordinary stones to me.'

Dud was taking apples from his pocket and did not reply till he was sitting at Bertie's side on one of the largest boulders. 'That's because you have not read the history of the 'stones',' he said then. 'They are granite, quarried at Mestlake — twenty miles away. It is fascinating to realise the difficulties which must have faced those early builders. Imagine bringing the rock all that distance . . . '

Dud was speaking very slowly but was so absorbed in his subject that he did not falter over one word. Bertie exclaimed, 'But, for goodness sake, why bring the stuff all that way? Wouldn't it have been easier to build nearer Mestlake?'

The man gave his slow smile. 'They didn't do things the easy way then. A company of monks landed from France at Riley Chine and their leader was taken ill as they began to prospect for a place to settle. Then their prior died here — and here they decided he must be buried, so of course this was the natural site for their monastery . . . Actually very little is known about it, for Henry the Eighth was instrumental in closing it. Records it contained were burnt and most of its granite looted for other buildings.'

As he stood up and lifted Nesta on the pony's back, Dud gave a rueful grin. 'Sorry . . . But you started me off yourself.'

Bertie smiled up at him. 'I'm very interested,' she told him. 'I daresay you could even show me the boundaries of the abbey. You must one day.'

He did not speak till they had gone some distance. Then all at once he said,

'No one has ever s . . . seemed to understand. They think I'm crazy. I s . . . see you don't. Th . . . thank you.'

With a little impulsive movement Bertie put her hand on his sleeve.

'One day you'll find something exciting, Dud, and that'll show them,' she exclaimed.

When they left the common they came to a stony road which eventually petered out in a narrow path sloping gently down towards the sea — though that could not be seen till they actually reached it, for their way wound between high, tree covered cliffs. It was Dorothy who, a little ahead of them all, caught the first glimpse of blue.

'It's lovely — lovely!' she cried.

It was. Golden sand stretched before them. Beyond it was the sea, a sparkling expanse of turquoise, which broke in foaming, booming waves.

Bertie said, 'I can't wait to get my shoes off and into the water. Come on, nips!' Then she paused. 'But we ought to see to the pony first . . . '

'I'll do that,' Dud told her. 'I can tether him back among the trees.'

David and Nesta pulled off their sandals and, hand-in-hand, raced for the sea — but in a moment they were back again. 'It's cold,' they said in chorus, while David added, 'Can't we have something to eat? I'm hungry.'

'You'll have to wait for Dud,' Bertie replied, 'he has the bag with all the food.'

'I'll go and meet him,' the small boy announced. Moments later Bertie heard him shouting and saw that he was riding now on the man's shoulder. Dud's expression was as happy as David's.

Bother, she thought, why did I have to do anything to spoil this grand day? He won't look like that if Bill and Marcia do turn up . . .

Then she pushed the thought away as Dud handed her a large bag saying, 'If someone else is hungry, so am I. Let's have our picnic while we have the beach to ourselves.'

Deliberately Bertie sat facing the approach to the sands and they had hardly finished their meal when she caught sight of a familiar tall figure.

Bill ploughed across the loose sand towards them and, with his hands in his pockets stood gazing down at them. 'You look a real family party,' he said. 'Mother and father and three children!'

Dud did not look at Bill. The expression that Bertie always called 'wooden' was on his face as he got to his feet. He did not speak but when he glanced at David the small boy scrambled up and the two went off towards a point of the cliff to the left which reached almost to the water. A moment or two later they had disappeared from view.

Bill flung himself down on the sand. He looked at Bertie. 'What's the idea?' He demanded. 'Dud Lambourne is the last person I'd have expected you to inflict on me.'

She did not answer at once.

Then she said quietly, 'He was good

enough to offer helping me with the children. We came over the common.'

Bill picked up a handful of sand and let it run through his fingers. 'You seemed all keyed-up and mysterious when you asked me to come. I thought it might even be you had managed something about Marcia.' He gave her a quick, wry look. 'I never imagined the mystery was — Dud. Anyway, how about a bathe? Coming in?'

Bertie shook her head. She certainly felt keyed-up now — expecting any moment that Marcia *might* arrive.

'It's too cold,' Nesta volunteered, picking up the spade Dud had provided. 'Please help me to build a castle.'

Bill laughed. 'I'm having my swim,' he announced. 'That's what I came for.' He pulled off his shirt and began to get out of his flannels. A moment later he was running down across the beach — a well-knit, muscular figure in red swimming trunks — and not for the first time Bertie thought — he's good to look at . . .

She saw him plunge into the water and then strike out into the sea. She was still watching his bobbing head when Marcia's voice spoke behind her.

'Hullo — I have come. Are *you* going to swim?'

'No.' Bertie was afraid that Nesta might reveal that Bill had just gone in and that Marcia would retreat. That was not in the plan.

Bertie said quickly, 'I think it's cold but if you don't mind that's up to you. I'd rather not myself, though.'

Marcia was already slipping out of a button-through frock and stood, lissom and lovely, before with a sudden movement she pulled a cap over her curls and then raced for the water. Bertie stood up. Far out she could see Bill's head. Surely Marcia must see it too . . .

Suddenly her gaze came back to the other girl and panic surged through her. She realised that Marcia had entered the sea very near a jetty where a large notice proclaimed DANGER. Was it

112

bravado on the girl's part or had she not seen the announcement? Bertie rushed down to warn her — but she was too late. In horror she saw that Marcia was caught in an eddy and was helpless.

Bertie glanced round, feeling helpless herself. To go in would only complicate things more, for she could not swim a stroke — yet she must do something. She began to shout, 'Bill! Bill!' But despair gripped her. How could she make him hear? The sound of the waves breaking on the shore was like thunder, overwhelming her puny voice. She must get help — but where? She was alone on the sands except for Nesta.

She turned and in that moment someone rushed past her. Bertie caught a glimpse of Dud as he plunged towards Marcia.

'Don't let him drown — God, don't let him drown.' Bertie's lips formed the silent words. 'Don't let him drown.' It was almost as an after-thought that she added, 'Let him save

113

her. Oh, let him save her.'

It was probably only minutes before Dud was back on the beach with Marcia's limp form in his arms. To the watching girl it had seemed hours.

'Oh Dud,' she whispered, 'she's not . . . ' He shook his head as he laid Marcia down. He was breathing in great gasps, yet his movements were calm and efficient. He obviously knew what he was doing as he began to apply artificial respiration.

Bertie did not even realise that Nesta and Dorothy had come to the water's edge and were watching with wide-open, frightened eyes. Her own gaze was on Dud's intent face.

'Here, let me take over . . . ' Bill had come on the scene unheeded by any of them. Immediately Dud surrendered his task to the other young man and almost at once there were signs that Marcia was returning to consciousness. When she opened her eyes Bill was bending over her. She breathed his name, uncertainly at first — then fully aware of him she exclaimed, 'Bill! Oh, Bill, my dear . . . '

Bertie had not planned a near-drowning to achieve a reconciliation between these two — but she *had* schemed for them to meet with that object in view.

'Marcia . . . Oh, my love . . . '

Blindly Bertie turned and made her way up the sands. Then she heard Bill's voice just behind her. 'Will you give me a hand with drying Marcia? She needs a good rubbing. Give me my towel, Bertie.'

She did as he ordered and, picking up the big towel Marcia had brought herself, she began the task of bringing warmth back into the other girl. It was not till Marcia was sitting with Bill's jacket round her, apparently little the worse for her adventure, that Bertie remembered Dud. How wet he must be — he had gone into the water partly dressed . . .

That thought sent her to look for him and as she reached the foot of the cliff she glanced back. Bill's arm was round Marcia now, her fair hair was pressed close against Bill's unruly black mop . . .

Was it wicked to feel so terribly jealous of Marcia's prettiness? Abruptly Bertie turned into the cliff path and gave a little whistle. Joe heard at once and came hurtling towards her. Then he turned to scamper back the way he had come. She knew he had gone back to Dud and a moment or two later she came on the man behind a huge boulder. She said quickly, 'You must be terribly wet.'

'N . . . not very. I've wrung my trousers out . . .'

'And put them back on?' she interrupted. 'Dud, you'll catch cold.'

'You can't catch cold from sea water.'

She looked into his serious brown eyes. Bill might have said that teasingly. Dud was in utter earnest. She smiled suddenly. 'All right. If you believe that it may be your faith will keep you immune! But you must be mighty uncomfortable.'

'N . . . no. I'm tough. I'm used to getting wet and staying all day in the fields sometimes — and that's not sea water, either.' Bertie was hardly listening now. A sudden wave of indignation had swept over her and now found vent in quick words. 'Dud, Bill is taking the credit for Marcia's rescue. It was *you* saved her.'

The man gave a slow smile. 'I'd not want her to know,' he said. 'And didn't you arrange this for them to make up? You . . . ' He broke off, and all at once it was impossible for her to meet the candid gaze of his eyes. She asked, 'Where's David?'

'Not far away — he's very excited by what we havc found.'

She smiled then. 'You and David are pretty good pals, aren't you?' she remarked.

When David appeared above them she called, 'Come on, let's go and get a drink. We have heaps of tea and orangeade in the bag.'

They were almost back to the others when David overtook them and in his shrill voice announced, 'Look at the lovely fossils I've got. Dud showed me how to find them.'

Bertie caught the supercilious glint in Marcia's blue eyes as their glance swept over Dud before she turned to Bill and gave a little laugh. Her tone was low as she spoke to him, but it carried clearly to Bertie who knew that Dud, too, was near enough to hear. 'That's appropriate, isn't it? Dud's an old fossil himself.'

Bertie bit her lip to keep back the indignant words that threatened to leap to Dud's defence. They would only amuse Bill and embarrass Dud. Best to stay quiet . . . But she felt a twinge of disappointment. *Bill* could have spoken in Dud's favour. Bill could have told that Dud was a brave man — but he did not.

Bertie saw Dud bend to say something to David and the small boy came towards them. 'We're going up — Dud and me — to see to the pony.'

Bertie said, 'The wind is blowing up. We ought to make for home. Bill, you must take Marcia back — she's shivering. Perhaps she should go to the hospital.' She stood up. She was longing to start homewards. She wanted to get away from the sight of the caresses which Bill and Marcia were exchanging quite openly. She wanted to get away from the tenderness in Bill's eyes — a tenderness which she herself would never be able to arouse.

6

Every time Bertie went across the common she was listening for Rusty's deep bark, hoping to see Bill's tall figure coming towards her. Surely, surely he would say thank you for her part in bringing him and Marcia together. Surely she was not unreasonable to expect that small crumb from him. Fool that she was to want to hear his voice — even if it was only of another girl he talked! Yet even that she was denied. Bill did not come. Most probably he was too occupied now with Marcia. Possibly the recent break between them had merely deepened the bond that now held them . . .

She topped the rise one day and, for a brief moment, knew a thrill which changed immediately to disappointment. Someone *was* approaching her — but it was Dud, not Bill. She began to move slowly down across the knoll towards him and as they met she asked, 'Have you been digging in the ruins?'

He nodded.

'Found anything?' she asked and now he shook his head.

'I can't think how you have the patience to go on,' she said, 'moving rubble time after time and hoping to find something that is very probably not there.'

He smiled. 'Patience and hope,' he answered quietly. 'Almost everyone has hope for their own special ambition or hobby . . . And everybody lives on hope.'

'*Everybody?*' she questioned.

'A good many folk hope for Paradise obtained by a win on the pools — just a few for the satisfaction of creating something perfect . . . ' He paused. That had been a long speech for Dud.

'Neither of those would be Paradise for me,' she told him.

'Wh . . . what would be?' he queried. But she could never tell him. She could never tell anyone. Paradise would be Bill in love with her . . .

She did not reply. Instead she stated, 'You don't go in for the pools and you don't spend your time trying to create something — so?'

'I'm hoping to find something — like you said . . . ' He was looking away from her and all at once began to move across the heather.

'What's the matter?' Bertie asked, beginning to follow him, and Dud pointed.

The girl saw him drop hastily to his knees. When she reached him he was holding a small bird in his hands.

'What is it?' she asked.

'A lark.'

'Oh . . . ' She gazed down at the streaky-brown little creature cradled in the man's large hands. She said, 'It has never been a bird to me before — but only a voice in the sky over the common.'

'This is not a voice any more,' he said. 'I've never heard one sing unless it

122

was in the air . . . ' He paused, gently caressing the small head with a couple of his fingers. 'This is just — a — lark with a — broken wing.'

Bertie held out her hands. 'Give it to me,' she ordered. 'It must sing again.'

'What can — you do?' Dud asked, but he obediently surrendered the bird. Joe jumped excitedly around her and Bertie said, 'You can do something, Dud. Take Joe home for me . . . '

'What are you going to do with the bird?'

'Take him to Dr. Newbury,' Bertie announced.

'You c . . . can't d . . . do th . . . that. He's a d . . . doctor not a v . . . vet.' It was a long time since she had heard Dud stammer so badly. She said, 'Dr. Newbury won't eat me. You go on home with Joe.'

After a short pause the man obeyed her. She watched him move away, followed by Joe.

When she got to the top of the lane Bertie hesitated. But she *couldn't* go to the front entrance of Turbary Grange. Quietly she unlatched the side gate and slipped into a wide bricked yard. She expected Rusty to bark and bound towards her, but everything was quiet. Quickly, before her courage should evaporate, she approached the back door of the large house. To her surprise it was Dr. Newbury who appeared in answer to her knock.

'I saw you coming across the yard . . . '

'Oh yes — and I'm glad it's you I'm seeing,' Bertie put in. 'Look, this lark was out on the common. It's got a broken wing. You must do something.'

'My dear girl!' The doctor's expression was fierce beneath his thick dark eyebrows. 'How dare you bring *that* here! I am a doctor.' Dud had said the very same thing, but Bertie had no fear now as she looked down at the injured bird and then up at the man. She asked, 'Didn't you realise what I said just now? This is a *lark*. You must have heard it sing — out there behind your house. If you won't do anything yourself — at least tell me what I can do. I don't know anything about broken limbs — except that I've heard they put a splint on a leg or an arm in a sling. Surely I can do something like that for this poor wee accident victim.'

The man stood looking at her. 'Whoever heard of putting a splint on a bird,' he muttered, more to himself than to her. But all at once he turned. 'Come inside,' he ordered. 'Stay here in the conservatory. I can't have *that* in my surgery.'

When Dr. Newbury returned he had a roll of bandage in his hand. He said, 'You won't have heard perhaps that, in an emergency in the event of a broken leg, it is possible to use the other leg as a splint. We'll try something like that for your lark.'

Minutes later Bertie was on her way home with her precious burden. When she reached the house next door Mr. Fawley came along his path towards her and, leaning over his gate, asked,

'Whatever have we here?'

Bertie explained and added, 'I'll keep it in a box in the shed for a while. Tied up like this it will not be able to fly, but in the end it will be all right.'

'I hope so.'

Bertie thought, looking down at the bird, But Mr. Fawley doesn't really think it will get better. Nobody except me believes it will . . .

Then abruptly she glanced up at her neighbour. He was saying, 'Marcia is engaged to Bill, you know.'

'Is she?'

'Yes, Mrs. Fawley thinks they are too young.'

'How old are they?'

'Twenty — both of them.'

Older than herself, Bertie was thinking as she went on indoors.

Her days were full, but the thought of Bill was always in the background of her thoughts, like a timpanist's instruments in an orchestra — sometimes soaring to an overwhelming volume, often muted to a thin thread of sound.

But he belonged to Marcia now . . .

That couldn't stop her loving him, though. She spent as much time in the garden as she possibly could. Always when she was in the house she had a feeling of confinement.

One day Mr. Fawley came to her hedge and, looking over, said, 'There's a lot of white butterflies about this year — see them across there! You'll be finding caterpillars eating up all your winter greens if you are not careful.'

Bertie made her way to the cabbage patch and then gave a quick exclamation. 'There are dozens and dozens here. What shall I do?'

'Pick 'em off,' he said laconically.

'Oh but . . . ' As she paused he chuckled. 'Get the twins to help you,' he told her.

Bertie was doubtful of the idea of getting the children to pick off caterpillars, but when she told them she would pay twopence a dozen for the small wriggly creatures, they were only to eager to help.

'Make good food for your skylark too,' the man had said. 'I looked it up in my encyclopaedia — they eat huge quantities of worms and insects.'

It was Saturday afternoon. For a while they all worked in silence. Then David shouted suddenly. 'Oh!'

'What's the matter?' Bertie asked.

'It's a furry one I found,' he replied, 'but something funny happened when I said 'Oh'. Nesta, you come and try it. Bend over and make a noise.'

Nesta, suspecting a trick, refused to obey and it was Dorothy who followed the boy's instructions. Straightening with a chuckle, she said, 'Oh, it *is* funny. You try.'

The older girl gave a big, 'Oh.' Nesta, close beside her, watched the insects. There were dozens of them all over the leaves. At the sudden sound above them they all stood up on end, dropping back in unison after a second or two. All three children found this great fun. Catching the caterpillars was forgotten in the excitement of the new game.

Even Bertie herself added an occasional loud 'boo' to the commotion in the cabbage patch. They were all so intent on seeing the insects standing to attention that they did not know anyone was approaching till a voice spoke over the hedge. Bertie straightened and looked into Dud's amused eyes.

'You'll think we are all crazy — especially me!' she laughed. 'We are supposed to be saving the cabbages from destruction and all we are doing is to worry a lot of poor caterpillars by booing at them!'

His face crinkled into a smile. Then he asked, 'Can I leave something here?' As Bertie moved towards the hedge he added, 'It's a perfect cresset stone. I've been digging in the Abbey ruins . . . '

She had no idea what a cresset stone might be but she went with him to the shed, where she told him he was welcome to leave it.

'See,' he enthused, 'it has sixteen holes. It's a kind of lamp that the monks used before they had candles.

They filled those holes with oil and put wicks in them . . . ' For some minutes he spoke, telling her the history of lamps. In his interest he was talking quite quickly, though occasionally he stumbled over a word.

When he stopped she said, 'We'd better cover it up with a sack or something. You make it sound like a rare treasure!'

'Oh, I don't suppose it's valuable — not as far as money goes — but there aren't many specimens in England. I'm not sure there is another as large and perfect as that.' He paused, looking at her. 'I'd like to get a man to look at it. That's why I wanted to leave it here. W . . . would you mind if I brought someone here?'

The excitement had died from his eyes and was replaced by that mute, imploring look she had caught the other evening. He did not like to admit how difficult his mother could be, but he was begging Bertie to understand without being told. Impulsively she put her hand for a moment on his arm.

'Of course we don't mind,' she told him. 'I'm glad you have not had all your digging for nothing — that you have found something worthwhile at last.'

'And the lark?' he asked then. She took him to the box where the bird sat looking very perky. 'Mr. Fawley said give him caterpillars — and it seems to have done him good,' she said ruefully. 'Is it silly of me, Dud? I just hate catching these poor little things — and as for feeding them to the bird — well, it seems rather horrible. After all, they are alive — just the same as the lark is . . .'

The man did not reply as he followed her out of the shed. He smiled as he went off along the garden path, and Bertie returned to the cabbage patch. She exclaimed, 'You won't earn much this afternoon if you don't work. Look, all the caterpillars you *have* caught are creeping out of your tins!'

That had the effect of starting operations again, but every now and again a loud 'Boo' echoed across the garden and Bertie had just added one of her own when she glanced up to see Bill and Marcia looking at her from outside.

Her face flushed as she caught the amusement in their eyes. She had not minded Dud seeing their childish fun. It was a different matter with the others. She hated to hear the teasing note in Bill's voice as he asked, 'Let us into this, will you? You seem to be having a good time . . .'

Ignoring his remark, she said quickly, 'I'll have to congratulate you both. Mr. Fawley told me . . . And now I must fly. I put a kettle on just now . . .'

Marcia had begun to raise her left hand, but Bertie simply could not stay and admire Bill's ring. She hurried till she reached the shelter of the house. It was true that there was a kettle on the gas, but only on a very low heat. Suddenly she sank into a chair by the table and buried her head in her arms.

'Oh, God, don't let it hurt so much . . . '

A day or two later she heard that Bill was going to London. Well, perhaps it would *not* hurt so much if she did not see him . . .

But she was to see him before he left Cordery. In answer to a knock on the door one evening she opened it to find Bill on the step. He had never been here before and she was too amazed at the sight of him to do anything except gaze at him. Her heart was thumping in a familiar way.

'Bertie,' he asked, 'will you help me?'

'Of course — I'd do anything for you,' she said breathlessly, and knew even as she spoke that once he would have laughed at her naivete — but now he was serious.

'I am going away to work,' he said. 'Will you take Rusty out for me?'

'Take Rusty out?' She repeated the words slowly.

Perhaps he thought she was remembering he was engaged to Marcia. He

133

said, 'It's no use asking Marcia to do it. You know how she hates the common when it's wet or rough. You don't mind. Of course I'll pay you. Dad even suggested I should get rid of Rusty but you know I couldn't bear that . . . '

As he broke off, the anger, which had flared in Bertie's heart when he mentioned payment, died away and she said quietly, 'Of course I'll take him out — but I won't let you pay me.' For a moment their glances met and held. She thought he was going to argue. Then all at once he put out his hand.

'You're a good sort, Bertie,' he said.

She went with him to the door and he told her to go in at the side gate of Turbary Grange. 'I don't expect you'll ever see anyone,' he told her.

As she watched him go off along the path she wondered if it was wicked to feel such a thrill at the idea of helping him. Well, he might be engaged to Marcia — but he had known where to come when he wanted a friend.

Joe ran past her towards the gate and

she followed him. Bill was going away and she wanted a last glimpse of him. She leaned over the wicket. She watched his tall retreating figure. He did not glance back, even when he turned the corner.

It was as she swung round to go indoors again that she saw the man coming from the opposite direction and, stopping, she waited for him. Joe had begun to bark in frantic welcome.

Dud reached the gate and stooped to pat the small dog. 'Joe d . . . doesn't f . . . forget me.'

'I wouldn't want him to forget you,' Bertie said quickly.

'No . . . no — because you're k . . . kind,' he said slowly.

'Were you thinking about Joe as you came along?' she asked. 'You had such a dreamy look on your face.'

'D . . . did I?' He was obviously startled by her perspicacity. 'I was dreaming about a rather w . . . wonderful idea.' He couldn't talk quickly but vividly he outlined for Bertie the big

135

ambition of his life. He wanted to have a large proportion of the ground at White Farm under glass. He would like to grow flowers and salad crops out of season. That way he could build up a flourishing concern.

'You could too,' she agreed, 'but you'd need capital to make a start with.'

He nodded as he made to go on.

'Why don't you take Joe with you and bring him in on your way back?' she suggested.

Dud smiled as she opened the gate, and he looked happy when he moved away with Joe jumping excitedly beside him. Bertie went slowly back along the garden path. It took so little to make Dud happy. For herself that would mean the attainment of the impossible — because never, never would Bill come to love her.

7

It was in November that Bertie had a letter from Bill. She read it twice before she could really take in what he had told her. He was going to New Zealand and he was writing to her about Rusty. He outlined two alternatives — that she might sell the dog or get him boarded out — 'on a farm or somewhere perhaps'. He had added, 'Though I always feel that my mother and father are safer with him there'.

Of course there was only one answer to that — she would go on deputising as long as she could. She fetched pen and paper to reply.

It was the first letter she had ever written to Bill, and for a long time she sat after writing her address, unable to put any more. She had to make what she said sound merely friendly — she must not let her heart show through her words, the heart that was saying now, 'Bill, you are going away to a country I can't even imagine — to fresh friends — but don't quite forget me. Oh, Bill, don't go . . . '

Stupid heart. He belonged to Marcia and *she* would have to let Bill go — very soon too. Bertie found herself reading his letter again.

'This is a chance I can't possibly miss. I am replacing a man who has been taken ill. The team he was in is sailing on November 16th, and I have to make a snap decision. I shall not have time to come home — pity — guess my mother and father will be a trifle upset . . . ' He did not mention Marcia. Would he see her before he went?

A couple of days later Dr. Newbury was waiting for her when she took Rusty back. Crossing the yard he put a hand on the dog's head as he looked at Bertie. 'You don't *want* to go on with this chore, do you?' he asked.

'I like doing it,' she said and then, 'I love Rusty.'

'Um . . . You're an odd child — ought to have been a kennel-maid — or a vet. Did that bird ever get better?'

'Yes — its wing mended quite all right. I have wanted to thank you . . . '

'Guess you felt a bit bad when it flew away?'

She nodded. His voice was gruff when he replied, 'But not quite so bad as we feel to have William flying off to New Zealand.'

'Perhaps he won't be gone long.'

'Several years, apparently. Can't think why *we* should have a son full of the wanderlust. But there, he's ambitious — wants to make a name for himself — building bridges instead of mending bodies . . . '

Once again Bertie felt he was talking more to himself than to her. He turned to go back into the house. She supposed he was taking it for granted that she *would* 'go on with the chore' of taking Rusty out.

She walked slowly as she left the side gate of Turbary Grange. She was kicking a pine cone — as she had done the very first time she walked along the lane and out to the common — the very first time she had ever seen Bill . . .

She did not see the man who was approaching her until he spoke. Then, in answer to his greeting, she looked up and said, 'Hullo, Mr. Fawley.'

'We had a card from Marcia this morning,' he said. 'She is in London. We were surprised.'

'Oh yes . . . ' Bertie hesitated before she asked, 'Did she mention Bill?'

'No, but of course we know he is working there — we guessed she had gone to be with him.'

Stupid to feel that it was impossible to say she had had a letter from Bill. She said, 'I have just seen Dr. Newbury. Bill is going to New Zealand.'

'No!'

'I expect Marcia will write and tell you so herself . . . '

Mr. Fawley chuckled. 'If I know the girl she has gone up there to persuade Bill not to go. It is likely she would succeed too. Marcia usually gets her own way.'

'Anyways,' Bertie said, 'I shouldn't like London in November.'

But as she left Mr. Fawley she was telling herself, 'What a fibber you are, Bertie Shefford. *You'd* like London in November if you were there with Bill — the same as *she* is.'

During the next days she went about the mundane tasks of the house automatically, not daring to let anyone know what she was feeling, not even able to vent her energy on her beloved garden because of the weather. In fact, just to look out at the sodden dead leaves had the power to depress her.

Only her trips over the common with Rusty and Joe were a relief to Bertie, for then she could talk about Bill to a sympathetic listener. The dog would look up at her with its great eyes alert whenever she spoke Bill's name, quivering beneath her touch as she said, 'But he's not here, old boy. He's going away — and we won't see him, either of us, for ages.' And she was sure that the animal understood as he licked at her hand, offering her comfort in his mute way.

November the fifteenth arrived and all through the day Bertie tortured herself with pictures of Bill and Marcia — together for this last day in England. Mr. Fawley might think Bill would allow himself to be dissuaded from this chance to fulfil his ambition. Bertie was sure no one could make him lose such an exciting opportunity.

When she went to bed it was not to sleep, but to see a liner drawing out from dock — and on board a figure she loved . . .

It was morning when the wild decision entered her head. She would go that day to Sotton. She would have a last glimpse of Bill before he went. She was up early, and when her father came down to breakfast she said, 'Dad, you don't mind if I go out today? There are some things I want — for the children.'

He gave her a quick glance, but she could never admit to her father what a crazy thing she was contemplating. She saw the expression which flitted into his eyes as he replied, 'No, I don't mind — but you'll want some money . . . '

'No,' she said quickly. 'I have never spent those saving stamps I had from Aunt Jane last Christmas.'

'But that is your money . . . '

She stopped his protests by saying, 'It's mine to spend any way I like, so please don't argue.' Then she went hurriedly out to the kitchen to make the tea. She called back, 'I'll leave you a cold lunch and let the three nips have theirs at school.'

She was ready very soon after the children had left for school and as she rushed out of the front gate she saw a man from one of the shops coming towards her in a van. 'Going to Scanlon?' he called.

'Oh yes!' This lift might mean she

could get an earlier train.

It was cold and as they neared the town a fine mist had formed, but she did not really notice it. All her thoughts were concentrated on getting to the station, and by a wild dash under the subway she managed to get the Sotton train almost as it pulled out.

To Bertie those miles would always be a memory of chugging wheels repeating over and over, 'Bill . . . Bill . . . Bill . . . ' and then rising to a quick cresendo, 'Bill is going . . . Bill is going.'

She sat crouched in a corner trying to see through the white mist which crowded close to the window, impatient every time the train halted at a station, but unprepared when eventually a porter called, 'Sotton. This is Sotton.' She had not realised that the port was so close for the fog had prevented any glimpse of ships in the docks. As she scrambled hastily to the platform her heart was thumping on the same word that had been the train's theme, 'Bill . . . '

Heedless of the cloying damp and cold, she made her way through the dreary streets, asking her way several times, wondering if she would *ever* reach the place where already a ship would be waiting to take Bill away. Then at the dock gates she found herself confronted by a policeman.

Almost as if by magic the mist had suddenly lifted and she could see the tops of two red funnels:

'The liner — when does she sail?' Bertie demanded.

'At noon, Miss.' The officer gazed down at her with serious eyes. She thought he was going to refuse her entry. She said breathlessly. 'It's my young man — I've come to see him off.'

'You've cut it fine, haven't you? It's half past eleven now.'

'I know — I couldn't get here sooner — I've come by train from Scanlon . . . '

'All right,' the man said then. 'Straight ahead.'

Bertie flew along the wide road that

seemed to stretch for miles ahead of her. She had fibbed twice over to that bobby — Bill was not *her* young man and she could not 'see him off' in the accepted translation of the phrase. All she hoped for was a brief glimpse of Bill.

She reached the wide quay and looked up at the huge ship which rode steadily beside it. Then she found a sheltered corner and stood scanning the decks. Surely Marcia would have gone aboard. Visitors did, didn't they? Visitors went over the ship, saw the cabins and all . . .

The sudden hooting of the vessel's siren startled her, and then she saw that people were coming down the gangways. Bertie watched each one, but she did not see Marcia. The dock was crowded now. Behind the rails of the liner was a solid mass of passengers.

Voices were sending last-minute messages back and forth from ship and shore — but she could not hear Bill's.

And then all at once she saw him. His

tall figure was unmistakable as he edged forward, looking out over the heads of those in front of him. From her position behind a small group of people, Bertie could see that his eyes were searching for someone — Marcia, of course.

Why wasn't she here?

Too absorbed in watching Bill to be conscious of the bustle aboard, Bertie did not realise that the gangway had been removed till, with another loud hoot of her siren, the ship began to move.

And still Bill's eyes searched. Vicariously she knew a surge of disapointment. To be leaving your country — with no sight of anyone who loved you to wish you luck ... Bertie was sure that Marcia had promised to come — but had failed him. And impulsively she herself moved forward — right to the edge of the dock. She waved her hands and shouted, 'Bill!'

She saw his answering wave, the surprise in his whole figure as he leaned forward. He waved again and again as the liner drew slowly away. Such a tiny strip of water divided them at first. She called, 'Good luck, Bill — good luck.'

That tumbling impassable waste became wider and wider till at last no sound would have carried either way. He, anyway, had not even called her name — but still her own lips soundlessly formed the words, 'Good luck, Bill, good luck.'

She stood there till mostly all the others had gone before she at last stumbled away. She had not realised how cold she was, but all at once she was shivering, and her legs were so numb that she might have been walking on wooden pegs. Her eyes were stinging with the tears she would not shed, even though they blinded her.

As she went out through the dock gates she did not realise the policeman was watching her, did not realise that she was turning in the opposite direction from which she came in. She was conscious only of the fact that she was so wretched in mind and body that she cared not at all where she went.

Then she felt her arm grasped from behind and turned to glance round. Still her vision was blurred and she saw the tweed of the man's jacket through a mist. She felt his hand tighten on her arm, his other one rested on her shoulder. Looking up she blinked away those betraying tears and then she gasped, 'Dud!'

He nodded but he did not speak. He simply led her away from the docks and into the warmth of a small restaurant.

She saw a trim waitress approaching and watched Dud as he deliberately laid the menu on the table and pointed.

Unpredictable Dud — he was the last person she would have expected to see here today. She asked falteringly, 'How did you know? I mean, did you come to the docks to find me? But you couldn't have — no one knew I was coming . . .'

He gave that slow smile of his. 'I knew Bill was sailing today — and y . . . you had a lift this morning. You were v . . . very anxious to catch a train.

I had to come to Sotton for some supplies.'

The waitress returned and put a bowl of steaming soup in front of Bertie. Oh, the comfort of that warming brew, and the satisfying taste of the meal which followed. Before it was over she felt warm. And, if her sense of desolation was not completely banished, at least she was able to tuck it unobtrusively into a corner of her heart.

Dud said, 'I came up by car — I'll take you back.' The thought of that lonely ride home by train had daunted Bertie. She said gratefully, 'Thank you.'

'I have some things to pick up,' he told her, 'but it won't take long.'

She asked, 'Could I buy shoes here — for the children I mean?'

He nodded. 'Know their sizes?'

'I have patterns of their shoes with me.'

'You'll get them cheaper here than in Scanlon,' he said practically. They left the restaurant, and Dud pointed out a large store on the opposite side of the road. He arranged that he would fetch his car, get loaded up with the goods he had come to fetch, and then return for her.

She watched him as he walked away from her and, as she had many times before, asked herself, 'Why do they call him *Dud*?'

And he seemed more sure of himself today than she had ever known. He was stuttering scarcely at all . . . though he had managed to get out of talking when he was in the café . . . but he was certainly no dud.

The thought was still in her mind as they started out for home. Dud drove in silence. Mist was coming down again, making it difficult to see far ahead, and as he concentrated on the road Bertie glanced sideways several times at his brown rugged face. What was he thinking beneath that impassive expression?

'I knew Bill was sailing today . . . ' That had told her more than a host of other words might have done. He *knew* that she cared for Bill. She said suddenly, 'You think I'm a fool for rushing up to Sotton today.'

Dud did not reply at once and she wondered if he was going to answer. Then, very slowly, he said, 'N . . . no. N . . . not if you care that much for Bill.'

A sudden lump in her throat made Bertie gulp, but after a moment she burst out, 'A fool then to care for him. Me — caring for him!' She gave another gulp. 'Dud, all Cordery would laugh at me if they knew. He's engaged to Marcia too. I *am* a fool to have done it. I've spent money on that journey which . . .'

When she broke off the man spoke quietly, 'We do foolish things when we let our hearts rule our heads. But it's good for us — perhaps.'

Bertie put out her hand and gave his sleeve a pat. 'Dud,' she said huskily, 'you are such a surprising sort of person. No one else would ever be so understanding. And yet they call you Dud — why?'

The question which had been at the back of her mind for so long had suddenly found vent in bald words. For a brief second he glanced round at her puzzled face. 'My name is Dudley,' he said.

The fog was thickening as they reached the river. The chill of it was seeping into the car. Yet all at once Bertie's hands felt clammily hot, and beads of perspiration stood on her forehead.

What a blundering stupid she was! She was the dud not to have realised there was an explanation as simple as that. Yet it had never occurred to her, and she had put the question in a way that could leave no doubt of the meaning she had read into his name.

All the man's concentration was needed now for his driving, and they crawled along very slowly. Then, as they climbed out of the valley, the fog thinned and Bertie saw him relax. She said, 'I *am* a little fool. You'll think it more than ever now.'

She was watching his profile and all at once saw the rare smile which touched his usually stern-looking mouth, and, though she could not see his brown eyes, she knew just how they would be dancing.

'No,' he said quietly. '*I* have heard how folk say my name. They think it's a joke. They think that, just because I can't talk as quickly as they do, my mind too is slow.'

'But it's not true,' she answered hotly. 'I have always known that — ever since the first time I met you. That's why I've often felt so angry when people . . . ' She broke off. In a minute she would be saying something else she'd regret.

His face was serious again and she went on, 'Dud, it's partly because you are so wooden with people. Why can't they see you the way I do?'

'Other folks' opinion has never worried me, Bertie.'

After that they did not speak for quite a long while. The November murk had turned to darkness by the time they reached Cordery and Bertie was glad she had told the children to go into Mr. Fawley's if she was not back by the time they returned from school.

She climbed rather stiffly from the car. 'Dud,' she said, 'it seems not enough to say just thank you, but . . . '

He was holding out to her the two shoe boxes she had left on the seat and as she took them she knew that he was trying desperately to find words to answer her, yet none would come. He was not usually at a loss with her . . .

She caught the sound of steps from the direction of the Fawleys' house. Then Mr. Fawley's voice called, 'That you, Bertie?'

'Yes,' she answered.

Dud drove away, but Bertie stood where she was and, reaching her, Mr. Fawley said, 'I heard the car stop and thought it was your voice. I wanted to catch you. We had a letter from Marcia today. She and Bill were married last week.'

PART TWO

1

Bertie was swinging her basket jauntily as she went along the road that day in early June. Golden chains of laburnum, masses of purple on rhododendron bushes, the honey smell of lupins . . . She wanted to sing and shout for joy. She did begin to whistle but stopped abruptly as she neared a low brick wall and found Mr. Fawley sitting on it.

'Are you all right?' she asked.

'Yes, I'm enjoying the sun — and a rest away from my womenfolk,' he replied.

There was no need to enquire how Mrs. Fawley was — she was never anything but ailing. Slowly Bertie remarked, 'Marcia hasn't got another job, then?'

'No, looks as though this time she is more than contented to stay. She gets a very comfortable allowance from Bill.' The man lapsed into silence, looking away from her and out across the fields opposite.

'She ought to go to Bill,' he added at last. 'That was the whole idea of his going to New Zealand, to make a home for her.'

'He said there were opportunities out there. He's done well, hasn't he?'

'Yes — he's been gone three years now, and last time he wrote he said he has a good job *and* a house. But Marcia doesn't seem in any hurry to pack up and go. Bill ought to stop her allowance is what I say. She's . . . she's . . . oh, it makes me mad to think about her.'

When, a moment or two later, Bertie went on she was no longer swinging her basket — nor was she whistling. Some of the glister had suddenly gone from the day. Very well Bertie knew what it was Mr. Fawley had failed to put into words. She knew the gossip which was being bandied around the village, tattle which linked Marcia's name with that of Tom Didcot, a married man.

As she passed the big house on the corner of Blacksmith Lane, Bertie found herself looking up at it. Sometimes she could even forget now that it had once been Bill's home. There was no doctor's plate on the gate now and a fairly new asphalt path led to a large conservatory that had been built only a couple of years ago. Bill would hardly recognise the place now.

Bill . . . Suddenly she was remembering him with painful intensity. At the beginning of his time abroad he had written to her in reply to her news about Rusty. Those runs every day across the common had been a great delight to Bertie, partly because she was doing what Bill had asked her in taking the big dog out.

She had gone in and out of the gate leading into the lane, and she had rarely seen either Dr. or Mrs. Newbury. Always Bill's mother had looked as though it would have been an easy task for a blustery wind off the common to pick her up and whirl her away. The doctor had been stocky with slightly bowed shoulders. He had appeared to be years younger than his wife. It was not till Bill went that he seemed to age. Once or twice, when Bertie met him, he confessed to being concerned over his wife's health.

Yet it was not she who had the stroke which separated them. Bertie knew she would never forget the day when she went in to fetch Rusty and found the old man fallen down in the yard. He had obviously been out to feed the dog. It was the last thing he ever did.

Bertie had been distressed and worried for Mrs. Newbury. She could remember even now the thrill which had gone through her when the old lady said, 'Bill will have to come home.'

But he did not come. He had been away only a matter of months. He would have had to find his fare and that he apparently could not do. His mother went into a nursing home. The house on the corner had only been rented by the Newburys, and it was sold.

Bertie cabled to Bill about Rusty. His reply had been. 'He is yours. Do what you like.'

But she could not take the dog home — already they had Joe. She went to Dud with her problem.

'I can't have him here at White Farm — you know that — but I'll think of something,' he had said. He had found a home for Rusty on a farm miles away and on the day that she said goodbye to the big dog she felt that her heart was breaking. She would miss Rusty rather badly — and his going snapped her one frail link with Bill. He wrote to thank her for all she had done, but she had never heard from him since.

Now she shook back her head as she went on towards the shops. What use to recall the old days? She wasn't unhappy. Her life had settled into a routine that was pleasant enough — and she was always busy. The twins were eight and full of energy which made plenty of work in the shape of mending and making clothes, to say nothing of the constant cleaning and tidying up after them. Dorothy now was eleven and an enthusiastic member of the Youth Club.

Bertie was thinking of the children as she went in through the door of The Cosy. Nesta and David had told her they wanted pencils and paintbrushes.

She was dazzled by the brightness of the day outside and could not for a moment see clearly.

'Hullo Bertie.'

She looked at Lily who added, 'Dim in here, isn't it?'

'It's just for a moment after coming in,' Bertie replied. 'Where's Dad?'

'Gone to the wholesalers. Do you want him specially?'

'No. I have come for some coloured pencils.'

Lily turned to reach down a box from a shelf behind her and, watching, Bertie noticed not for the first time how plump the other girl was getting. All at once she seemed to have changed from a scrawny child into a buxom young woman. As she put the box of pencils on the counter she looked at Bertie. 'Has your Dad told you about our plans?' she asked.

'Plans?'

'There, I can see he hasn't but I expect you will agree with me that it *is* about time we had a change round here. First of all we'll have those wooden backs taken out of the window and have glass instead. That will give us more light in the shop. And the counter is going over there . . . ' Lily outlined the proposed alterations.

'Now we have Jane here we need more room and the rearrangements will give it to us,' she ended.

'Whose idea is all this?' Bertie asked. 'Not Dad's?'

Lily laughed. 'Your Dad would be content to go on in the same old rut for ever!'

'Dear old Dad — but it looks as if you are waking him up, Lily.'

After Bertie had paid for her

purchases she still lingered for a moment, looking round and trying to visualise what the shop would be like after all the renovating that Lily had described.

During the time that Mr. Shefford had been here he had built up the business, more than doubling the takings and, finding now that he needed an extra assistant, had just taken on another young girl. The owners rarely came near the place and her father was virtually the boss. Bertie was glad that he had made a success of the job. As she went out into the sunshine again she was remembering how he had looked sometimes just after they came to Cordery — worried and thin. He had still not put on much weight but his was a healthy leanness now, and the hollows had left his cheeks. He looked happy too. The debt which had fretted him in those early days was now paid off, his grief over her mother's death had dimmed.

It was a day or two later, as they

finished their mid-day meal, that Jack Shefford said, 'Bertie, will it be all right if I ask Lily to tea on Sunday?'

'Lily! Yes, I suppose so. Is she going to be alone or something at the weekend, and so you feel you must take pity on her?' Lily had never been to tea before and Bertie was surprised by her father's suggestion.

'No . . . No, it's just that I want her to come. You like her, don't you?'

'Yes, of course.' She looked at her father and now her surprise was tinged with sudden unreasoning foreboding. Jack Shefford was obviously ill-at-ease. He was avoiding her eyes.

He said after a long pause, 'Bertie, I am going to ask Lily to marry me. I'm not sure she will have me but . . . ' As he broke off Bertie said unevenly, 'Dad, I don't know what to say. I never guessed. She is so — young.'

'But she has a shrewd head on those young shoulders. She's as sensible as a woman twice her age and we . . . we get on so well together. *I* don't feel there is all that gap in the years between us.' He picked up his glass of water, sipped it and put it down again.

Bertie said, 'I'll go and make the tea — the kettle will be boiling.'

The children had already gone off to school. Always Bertie and her father had a cup of tea before he returned to the shop, and always she had enjoyed this ten minutes when they exchanged gossip and confidences. But she had not really been much in his confidence, she thought. He had never given her a hint before about how he felt over Lily.

She brought two cups of tea from the kitchen and put them on the table.

'Bertie, I don't want anything to be altered as a consequence. Lily will still keep on her work at the shop . . . '

And I can go on being the home drudge . . . That thought startled Bertie. To work for Dad had never seemed drudgery. She looked at him. But suddenly they were strangers.

He didn't want anything altered. Of course it would be. Lily coming in here to be stepmother to the twins — and Dorothy. To herself!

All these years she had felt wanted. Now she would not really be needed. Lily would be unlikely to want her here. She asked, 'Have you told the others?'

'No, of course not. I wanted you to know first. I thought you might want to tell the nips yourself.'

'Oh no!' She spoke quietly. 'I think you must do that, Dad,' she paused. 'How soon — will it — happen?'

'Oh, not for a little while. Remember, I haven't asked Lily yet.'

'But you are pretty sure of what the answer will be?'

'Yes — fairly sure — and once I have asked her I wouldn't want to wait too long. Bertie, you don't mind?'

'No — it is your life, Dad.' She hoped she did not sound bitter, but she simply could not infuse any warmth into her voice. She could not even wish him well — not yet.

After he had returned to work Bertie stood for a long time at the window.

Now that he was gone she was finding it difficult to *believe* what he had said.

Lily . . . Her father's voice echoed back across the years. 'She's such a quaint little piece.' He had found her so amusing when he first went to the shop — but even then she had started to make rearrangements. 'We'll have a new rule.'

Bertie turned slowly and looked round at the room, trying to see it with the eyes of a stranger — Lily's eyes. Suddenly she could hear Lily's voice talking about the 'rearrangements *we* are making in the shop.' Bertie hadn't noticed the 'we' then. And here? Surely Lily would want to make changes here.

Dad and Lily . . . of course they were together a lot in the shop — but that they should marry . . .

Slowly Bertie moved and began to clear the table. But once in the kitchen she was activated by the urge to get out of the house — this house where, for four years, she had been sole mistress.

She whistled for Joe and, leaving by

the side gate, made her way along the track which led to White Farm. She had no conscious aim in going that way. Her only idea had been to get into the air where she could think.

She went along the path which bordered the outside of Dud's farm. Joe scampered into the trees at her right, burrowing among mounds of pine needles — left by children who had played in the woods — and then racing back to drop a cone at her feet. This was the game which had been Joe's first introduction to Bertie and he never tired of it.

But automatically today Bertie kicked the pine-cone for him to chase after. She walked on, breasting a small knoll and emerging into a lane hedged by brambles. She turned left and still she was on the boundary of White Farm, yet she was so immersed in her own concerns that she did not see Dud till he spoke — from the other side of the hedge.

'Oh — hullo,' she said, looking up

and at the same moment catching the glint of sunshine on a fairly large expanse of glass. 'I believe you have had some greenhouses put up!' she exclaimed.

'Yes, I am going to try growing flowers and tomatoes. It's something I've always wanted to do.'

'I remember you telling me about that ambition ages ago. And now it is coming true. Have you been left a fortune?'

'No.' He gave his slow lop-sided grin. 'I have been saving up. I have only just got enough.'

'You plan to *make* a fortune then!'

'I don't expect so. In fact, if I'm going to do anything much I'll have to get help and I don't know how I'll do that.'

'For one thing because you'd hate having a stranger around?' she suggested.

'Partly,' he agreed.

'Then suppose you take *me* on?'

'Y . . . y . . . you. B . . . b . . . but . . .'

It was a long time since she had heard him stammer like this.

'Dud, if you don't want me say so — I won't mind. Because of course I have no experience, but I'm willing to learn — if you think you could teach me.'

'You'd learn easily enough,' he told her. 'But how about your own job?'

'Of looking after the family? I'll manage all right. The children are bigger now.' For a moment she was tempted to tell him about her father and Lily — but suppose it did not happen?

After a long pause she asked, 'When can I start?'

'Whenever you like — tomorrow . . . '

'Thank you, Dud — I came out feeling so miserable but you have cheered me up no end.'

'Miserable?' he asked and she nodded. 'I'll tell you about it — but not now . . . ' She hesitated. It was Thursday. There were things she would need to do before Sunday. When Lily came she should find the house as shining and bright as soap and water, polish and Bertie Shefford could make it. And Lily should have for her tea the home-cooked cakes and pastries that Dad loved.

Bertie said, 'I'd like to start at the beginning of the week. Can I come on Monday?' He nodded and she made to go on. Then she paused.

'Dud, I . . . I don't think Mrs. Lambourne likes me . . . ' And that was a mild way of putting it!

Between them suddenly were the occasions when Mrs. Lambourne had shown her dislike of Bertie — that first time of all when Joe had been taken to White Farm — and afterwards the older woman's hostility had seemed to grow with every meeting.

Dud said, 'You won't see her. She hardly ever leaves the house now.'

'Why — is she ill?' Bertie asked quickly.

'It's her heart, I think, but she won't have a doctor.'

The girl caught the concern in his brown eyes. 'I'm sorry, Dud,' she said quietly. No matter how Mrs. Lambourne might seem to an outsider, she was Dud's mother. He said slowly, 'She's worked hard, Bertie — too hard often.'

2

That Sunday Bertie tried not to let her father see how very much she hated the thought of Lily coming. Always there had been a special bond between her and Jack — a bond which seemed to have snapped when he said, 'I'm going to ask Lily to marry me.' Instead now a barrier of constraint had been raised, and Bertie felt cut off, alone in a friendless wilderness. If only the gap in the ages of herself and Dorothy had not been so large — so that she could have talked things over with a sister — but Dorothy was too young. And Bertie had made no close friends in Cordery . . .

It was a sunny afternoon. As soon as the children had gone off to Sunday School their father stood up. He said abruptly, 'Well, I'll go and fetch Lily.' He did not glance back as he went through the doorway. She watched him go and then began to lay the table.

She had just finished when she heard footsteps on the path, then Lily's laugh intermingling with her father's deep tones. They came in. There was no hint of self-consciousness about the girl, but the man was showing an unease that Bertie had never seen before.

Perhaps he was afraid his daughter's welcome would lack warmth. Well, he need not have worried.

Lily was carrying a large bunch of tulips which she held out to the other girl.

'Oh, they are lovely!' And Bertie's surprised delight was not simulated. 'Our daffodils are just over. Dad, take Lily out to see the garden while I put these in water. They will look beautiful in the middle of the tea-table.'

And then the twins came running in, pleased with the sweets brought by their visitor, but obviously rather envious of the box of chocolates given to Dorothy who followed them. They had always known Lily — almost as part of the

shop — but never as part of their
father's private life. Yet now they
accepted the girl easily, especially when
she showed herself eager to join in their
games of 'I spy,' and 'Noughts and
crosses.' They were even more pleased
when she taught them games they had
never heard of before.

Lily stayed till after the twins had
gone to bed. Then Jack said he would
walk home with her. After they had
gone Dorothy said, 'She's fun, isn't she?
Why hasn't she ever been here before?'

That was a question Bertie was not
prepared to answer . . . Quite obviously
Lily had charmed all three of the
children, but would they be so keen to
accept her as their father's wife?

Dorothy's bedtime came and she
went off upstairs. Bertie sat trying to
read. She turned pages but afterwards
she could not remember anything. Her
eyes had seen the words but their
meaning had not penetrated her mind.
She was waiting . . . waiting for her
father's return.

Having seen him with Lily today there was no doubt at all in her heart of the position between them. Once she had escaped into the garden on the excuse of fetching a towel from the line, but only really to escape the affection-ate glances passed from one to the other. To Bertie there had been something almost indecent in the obvious affection of her father for this plump girl — in the way he called her 'Lil' with the intonation of a boy in his teens for his first love.

But perhaps it was only because of her memory of Mrs. Shefford. Dad and Mother . . . Now Dad and Lily — who was no older than Bertie herself. It all seemed so unbelievable. I've always loved Dad, but fancy marrying him! Can't Lily see he is old — too old for her?

It was late when Jack got home. He came into the living-room, blinking after the darkness outside, blinking perhaps to hide his embarrassment. As he walked across the room Bertie stood up. There was a long pause. Then he said, 'I asked Lil to marry me.' Another pause. 'Like myself, she doesn't want to wait too long.'

Bertie swallowed. She knew she had been trying to persuade herself that Lily would realise how incongruous was a marriage with such a discrepancy in ages — that Lily would say 'no.' Now there was no hope left. And she was to have a very short respite. She said, 'I hope it works out all right, Dad.' And knew that her father had been expecting something warmer than that. But why should she give it? Did he really think she would welcome Lily with open arms? Did he really believe in his own heart that it would work?

She said, 'I'll make your cocoa.'

'No,' he said, 'I won't want any tonight. Lily's mother made a drink before I left.'

Bertie turned abruptly towards the inner door. She felt a sudden constriction in her throat. Already things were changing. This was the first time in years that she had not made cocoa for herself and her father before going upstairs at night. She had waited to have her own till he came in. Surely he must have known she would wait, but he did not seem to think it odd she was not going to the kitchen to get a drink for herself. Anyway, she did not want it now.

But there was something she had to tell him. 'Dad, I've promised to go to work for Dud Lambourne. I'm starting tomorrow morning.' Just a bald statement of fact. Oh, what had happened to all the affection between them? She might have been speaking to a stranger.

The man looked at her. 'Bertie,' he began, and then broke off. She avoided his glance but she could not go to bed without an attempt to get back to a measure of their old pally footing. She said, 'Dud has got some glass-houses — he has heaps of work but can't get anyone to help, so I have offered to give him a hand. I don't know how I'll get on, but I've promised to try.' She hesitated. 'I'll be able to manage about meals and all.'

He moved across towards her, put his hands on her shoulders. 'Bertie, I don't want you to do this and overwork yourself — but if it is what you want to do . . . '

'It is, Dad.'

'All right, then.' He put his lips on her cheek. 'Goodnight, lass. God bless.'

'Goodnight, Dad.'

She went hastily up the stairs and let herself quietly into the room she shared with Dorothy. For a long while she lay, head burrowing into her pillow. Was it wicked of her to feel she hated Lily — wicked to blame her father so bitterly for the upheaval he was making — not only to her outward life, but inside her too?

The next morning she began work at White Farm. Dud set her first to prick out seedlings. She said, after he had shown her what to do, 'Dud, I'll work a specified time each day. Tell me how many hours you would like me to do.'

'How many can you spare?'

'I can start fairly early but I'd like a long break at mid-day so that I can get dinner for them at home.'

'Of course,' he agreed. 'I don't mind how you arrange your day. I'm only grateful to have you.'

So at dinner-time she had the meal ready when she heard voices outside, footsteps on the path. Dad and the children had arrived together. The halting of the scrunching feet told her they had reached the veranda. She could hear her father's voice.

A moment later the twins burst into the kitchen. 'Bertie, what do you know!' David shouted. 'Our Dad's going to marry Lily. She's coming here to live. Won't that be smashing?'

'She'll be able to play games with us *every* day,' Nesta broke in. Bertie's glance went to Dorothy who had followed her brother and sister. She expected that Dorothy would resent Lily's intrusion. Dorothy could remember Mum.

But the girl seemed to have no resentment at all. She said, 'Lily's going to have me and Nesta for bridesmaids. Isn't it exciting? Dad says we can have new frocks and Lily will make them.'

Never in her life before had Bertie felt so alone as she did at that moment. Before she went back to work she took Joe for a run, and then tied him up on a long rope which gave him quite a run of the garden. Joe hated this indignity but she could not risk him following her to the farm. He stood wagging his tail, his eyes looking up at her — showing so clearly his adoration.

'Joe . . . ' She fondled his ears. 'Joe, *you* never notice how plain and ordinary I am. You love me, even if nobody else in the world does.' When she moved away from him he gave a little whining cry. 'I'm sorry, old boy, but it's got to be this way. I'll give you a long run tonight,' she promised.

★ ★ ★

Bertie's willingness to learn gave added value to the experience she gained every day. Soon there was little she could not do on the farm. Quite obviously Dud did not want her to come into contact with his mother. Bertie noticed that never, on any account would he let her work near the house. In fact she spent a lot of her time in the glass-houses, and she found her tasks there absorbing.

One day Dud bought a job-lot of flower pots at a sale, and drove in with them just as Bertie arrived back after dinner. She said 'I'll help you unload them.'

'All right — they'll have to be washed too,' he told her. 'Can't use dirty pots.'

'Shall I do them?'

'If you don't mind the job. I do want to get some hoeing done.'

So Bertie began the task of washing those piles of earthy pots. She had not done half of them when she saw a man coming towards her. He was dumpy, with a round cheerful face, and he wore a clergyman's collar.

Bertie straightened. This would be Cordery's new rector — she had heard he was arriving, but this was the first time she had seen him. He said, 'I have come to find Mr. Lambourne.'

'He is hoeing,' she answered. 'I'll go and fetch him.'

'No, no. Tell me where to find him. I know farmers are busy men.'

'It's rather muddy across the fields,' Bertie protested, and the man chuckled.

'That will not worry me. I have lived on a farm.'

Still a trifle doubtfully she directed him — 'Round the pig sty, past the hay-stack and through the first gate.'

'Thank you.' The little man smiled. 'Before I go may I know who *you* are? You will be one of my parishioners and I want to be friends with you all.'

Bertie told him her name and where she lived. 'Ah,' he said, 'you are Mr. Shefford's daughter. I have already met your father, my dear.'

She finished her mammoth wash-day

and then went into one of the green-houses. With her whole mind on her job she forgot the visitor till Dud arrived. He was concentrating on flowers for the Christmas market — cyclamens and azaleas — and Bertie was fascinated by the hundreds of pots he tended with such loving care

As he moved towards her she said, 'Dud, don't you feel worried some-times, about these babies of yours? How do you know they will be out just when you want them to be — and not too early or too late?'

His smile came as he looked at the 'babies.' '*How* do I know? Well, you wait and see. They'll be ready just when I want them to be.'

He turned to glance at her. 'That clergyman you sent out to me . . . ' Dud paused, giving an unusual frown and Bertie imagined she might have done something wrong till he went on, 'He is sending his niece over to see me and you can guess how I am — not looking forward to that.'

'If she is at all like him I shouldn't think you need worry,' Bertie remarked. Then a sudden thought made her add suddenly, 'They come from a farm. Does she want to work for you?'

'Oh no! He came about the cresset stone in the church. She is interested in those sort of things. Actually she doesn't live with him, but is coming to stay at the rectory for a while.'

. Relief surged through Bertie. She was not very expert yet and was afraid her position might be usurped — but it had been a stupid idea to imagine the rector's niece would be looking for a job on a farm!

She smiled. 'If the woman is not here, she may never come — so — don't worry, Dud about an evil that may never happen.'

'Evil?' he repeated slowly turning away so that she could not see his face.

'Well, I don't know,' he added. 'It is nice for someone to be interested in the stone, but it's always a nightmare to me when I think of meeting strangers.'

Bertie was to remember that conversation and wish desperately that Eve Bampton had *not* come to Cordery. She was not very handsome and it was difficult to assess her age. Perhaps she was not much over twenty. She might be nearer thirty. She drove a little two-seater car and she wore a tweed suit.

She went first to see Dud one evening and he told Bertie about the visit next morning. His eyes were glowing as he said, 'She is really interested in the Abbey ruins and even thinks she can write about them in a book . . . '

'Why Dud — that's wonderful!' Bertie exclaimed.

'Yes . . . '

'And was meeting her such an ordeal?'

'It wasn't too bad. I think I'll get on with her all right.'

Bertie glanced at him. Of course, once he was off on the subject he had always been so interested in, he'd even forget about the woman who was listening. Bertie smiled. 'She'll be wanting to take a picture of you digging in the ruins.' There was a mixture of teasing and seriousness in her tone. 'That would make Cordery sit up . . . a picture of you in a book, Dud.'

She expected a denial of any such ambition, but to her surprise Dud did not reply. When she glanced at him his face was a dull red. One of her quick rushes of sympathy filled Bertie's heart. Poor old Dud . . . He was eagerly anticipating this fame for his beloved Cordery Abbey. Yet he didn't even know that Eve Bampton would get her book published . . .

★ ★ ★

Both her father and Lily had seemed to be in a hurry at the beginning but weeks were going by and the date was not fixed, though Lily was in and out of the house a lot. And talk seemed to be all about the wedding, the bridesmaids' dresses and the reception.

One day Bertie had only just got to the farm when she heard a sharp yelp, followed by a familiar whimper. Joe! He had managed somehow to get free. He had followed her. There came the lift of an angry voice, another yelp, and Bertie raced towards the sounds. She rounded a corner into the yard. Outside the back door of the house stood Mrs. Lambourne. Joe limped across towards his mistress and Bertie gathered him into her arms. Advancing slowly towards the other woman she demanded, 'Did you hit him?'

Mrs. Lambourne did not answer the question. 'You!' she exclaimed. 'I might have known — I was sure Dud was different lately. Get off my premises — and stay off.'

Bertie stopped at some little distance from the other woman. She was shocked by the change in Mrs. Lambourne. Dud's mother was still trim, but her face was like wrinkled parchment. Her body had shrunk to the size of a child's.

At that moment Dud came round the house from the opposite direction. He glanced from Bertie to the older woman, who swayed, putting out a hand to the door for obvious support. Hastily he moved to his mother who swayed again and would have fallen had not Dud caught her. Bertie saw him disappear into the darkness of the house and for a moment she stood undecided. She had never been inside Dud's home. She could not go now, even to offer her help. To go near the other woman would undoubtedly only excite her and make matters worse.

Bertie began to move across the yard. 'I'd better take you home, Joe,' she remarked. 'You are a naughty boy — making all that schemozzle.'

When she reached the lane she put him on the ground. 'Come on — home,' she urged. But Joe crouched still, whimpering, and again she lifted him into her arms. 'If she's hurt you I'll not forgive her in a hurry,' Bertie whispered walking as quickly as she could.

She took Joe indoors and put him into his basket, but he could not swivel round and round in his usual fashion before settling down. She stroked his head and he licked her hand.

She said, 'I'm going to shut you in for the afternoon. You'll be better by the time I come home won't you?'

When she got back to the farm she went straight to the glass-houses and it was there that Dud found her not long afterwards. He said, 'I'm s . . . sorry, B . . . Bertie. I s . . . should have t . . . t . . . told her you were here.'

He rarely stuttered now when he was talking to her. She knew he must be feeling very upset. Quickly she answered, 'It was partly my fault, Dud. I ought to have made absolutely sure Joe could not get off his rope. I'm sorry it happened.'

She paused, looking up at him. His face showed his obvious distress and she asked, 'How is Mrs. Lambourne?'

'I've put her to bed.'

'Dud, you said she was ill. I can *see* she is. Surely now you will send for the doctor.'

'I daren't, Bertie.'

'But you must. If you got the doctor here she would have to see him.'

'You don't know Mum. She told me only a minute or two ago that she doesn't want any doctor.'

'If only Dr. Newbury were here — you knew him. But I tell you Mrs. Lambourne *must* see some doctor.'

'I couldn't get anyone here against her wishes — I c . . . couldn't do it.'

Bertie felt suddenly angry with him. 'Dud, be a man,' she said hotly. He looked at her for a moment as though she had hit him. Then abruptly he turned away. She did not see him again for the rest of the morning.

3

It was one of those warm evenings that come at the end of a July day. Bertie was in the kitchen, making a cake. The others were in the garden and occasionally the sound of their voices drifted in to her, but Bertie did not realise Lily was there until a sentence reached her clearly. 'What have you got there, David?'

'A bird — it's hurt.' There was a pause before Lily said, 'Give it here — best thing is to wring its neck and put it out of its misery.'

Instinctively Bertie moved towards the window but in the same instant an exclamation from David halted her. 'Oh no!' he exclaimed. 'Lily, you horrid, cruel thing! Where's our Bertie? She's a wizard — she'll cure it.'

A surge of wild triumph ran through the girl in the kitchen. For the first time the charming Lily was tumbling off her pedestal and 'our Bertie' was in demand. But immediately Bertie felt ashamed. What did she want? For Dad's marriage to be a failure before it began? Of course the matter-of-fact Lily would see no hope for an injured bird — and her reaction had been to show mercy in the only way she knew.

Bertie made for the back door and met David just outside. He was holding a sparrow in his two hands. He said, 'Look, it's shivering but . . . ' As he hesitated Bertie took the bird from him. 'Poor wee creature,' she said, after looking at it, 'I should think perhaps a cat has mauled it a bit, and I believe it's more frightened than hurt. Come on, let's put it in the shed.'

As usual Nesta was on hand and danced round Bertie as she went towards the shed. Dorothy followed too, and it was quite a long while before they left the sparrow crouching in a box in the far corner.

'If it was a lot hurt so that we had to

look after it for ages — then perhaps it would stay with us always,' Nesta remarked thoughtfully as she watched her sister closing the shed door.

'Would you want it to stay for always?' asked Bertie. 'Don't you think it would rather have its own little companions?'

'I'd like a tame bird,' Dorothy put in, 'and you would think that *one* of all the lot we have rescued would let us make a pet of it. It seems so ungrateful to fly away — and not care about the trouble we have taken over it.'

'I suppose that's nature — you can't expect a bird to say thank you,' Bertie laughed. 'And now I'd better get back to my cake-making.'

But when she reached the kitchen she found that Lily had finished the cake and her round face beamed as she said, 'I thought you wouldn't want all this stuff wasted by being left, Bertie.'

Biting hard on her lower lip, Bertie choked back her sudden annoyance at what had seemed interference. After all,

Lily's words held no censure. The girl was just trying to help. Yet, for all that, Bertie could not help her resentment at seeing Lily in her kitchen, couldn't help being exasperated by Lily's obvious capability. It was a feeling which found vent in hot words when Lily said in obvious puzzlement, 'I can't think why you bothered with a sparrow. There are such hundreds of them and they are not even pretty birds. They are drab and they don't sing . . . '

'So just because they are plain little creatures you wouldn't mind wringing all their necks,' Bertie put in. 'That is a cruel inhuman way of looking at things. And I'll tell you this — if you don't like birds I don't think Dad is going to like you very much. In fact . . . ' She broke off and, turning away, went into the livingroom.

Her only thought, in that moment, had been to hurt Lily, but suddenly had come the realisation that to hurt Lily would be to hurt Dad as well.

Slowly Lily followed her and Bertie

saw the round, good-natured face crumpled into bewildered distress.

'I'm sorry,' Bertie said. 'I expect you think I'm a bit of a crank. Perhaps I am slightly cranky over anything that is hurt. Forget what I said, will you, please?'

Lily's smile came quickly. 'Heavens — we all have our funny ways,' she said. 'I have, I know, but we will make allowances for one another, won't we, Bertie? We must be good friends . . .'

But Bertie had no time to reply before she heard the sound of her father's familiar whistle and hastily Lily turned. 'Here's Jack,' she said, and rushed eagerly to meet him.

Jack — the man who had always been Dad till now. Bertie wondered if she would ever get used to hearing Lily speak to him in that way as — Jack.

Not many minutes later Bertie was alone in the house. Dorothy had gone off to spend the evening with Mandy Jones. Dad and Lily were going with the twins to the woods. They had just taken it for granted that Bertie would stay — cleaning, looking after the cake . . .

Sudden rebellion welled up in her heart. All the others were out. Why shouldn't she go too? So much now had to be crammed into her off-times. There were things she *ought* to do . . .

'Bust it all tonight,' she said aloud. 'Come on, Joe — you and I aren't going to be the only ones left out of the general exodus.'

But the little dog didn't answer her calls and whistles. Where was he? Had they taken Joe too?

Then she heard an odd little whimper and, stooping, looked under the table. The animal gazed at her with dull eyes and reached out his tongue, but he did not move his small body. Bertie knelt down.

'Joe,' she whispered in sudden heart-contracting concern. 'Joe . . . '

Her hands fondled his ears while desperately she wondered what she ought to do. Joe was ill, very ill — she could see that. But not dying — he could not be dying . . .

Yet even the thought sent a stabbing fear right through her heart — and there was only one person who would understand, only one person who loved Joe as much as she did herself.

Gently she picked up the little dog. How *thin* he was! She hadn't realised . . . Had she been too busy to look after him properly? Or was this the result of Mrs. Lambourne's attack on him? He had seemed all right after a couple of days — and she had not worried any more, but she ought to have taken him to a vet.

At any rate, no matter what the cause of Joe's illness, Dud would know what to do now. As she wrapped a piece of old blanket round the small body her throat felt dry and she could hardly speak. 'Joe, my poor little Joe . . . '

She dared not hurry along the rutty lane towards the farm for fear of jolting her small invalid, but her thoughts were jumping ahead of her feet. When she could get him to Dud it would be all right. Dud would know what to do . . .

She paused in the gateway of the farm. She could not possibly go to the door of the house. Anyway, Dud would most likely be out of doors. She knew he used every possible minute of daylight. After only a second or two she decided to make first for the greenhouses. He had been a bit worried today about several of his cyclamen plants — she would probably find him there . . .

All the glass had been whitened against the glare of the summer sun, so she could not see whether Dud was inside — but she must find him — soon she must find him. With her foot she began to push open the door, and then she stopped, drawing back. Dud was there — but he was not alone. At the further end of the glass-house she had caught a glimpse of Eve Bampton putting an arm across Dud's shoulder. Eve was not wearing the tweed suit this evening but a pretty summer frock. And Eve's voice was gay as it carried clearly to Bertie — 'Oh, you dear clever Dud . . . '

Automatically Bertie turned away. She felt bewildered. Dud, with Eve's arm around him . . . Suddenly came the memory of that first day he had talked about her — the look in his eyes — the dull red of his cheeks . . . but Dud!

Hardly realising what she did Bertie went back the way she had come. She felt as though caught in a thunderstorm on a hitherto sunny day. Always Dud had been there — till now.

Very slowly she walked along the path and indoors. Immediately she was assailed by a smell of burning. She had completely forgotten the cake. She opened the oven door and, turning off the gas, laid Joe on the mat in front of the cooker. If he got warm and would take some milk . . .

She took out the cake. Perhaps by and by she could scrape off the burnt part, but more important was to get some milk heated. When she had it ready she picked Joe up and sat down in front of the opened door of the cooker.

Then, with blurred eyes, she knew it was no good. Poor dear little Joe — even he did not need her any more.

4

Waking had regularly been a fascinating game to Bertie. The first drowsy realisation that morning had come — the sudden deliberate refusal to open her eyes until she had tried to guess what kind of day it was going to be, gauged by the amount of light to be seen through nearly closed lids — the delicious delight as she decided 'sunny' — the warm thrill of getting out of bed to draw the curtains so that sunlight on wall reflected in mirror and back to wall — the zestful thought of hours ahead to be filled with the care of her family and garden . . . But it was a game not to be played when you hated facing the day before you . . .

That morning she opened her eyes slowly. She was waking to her first day under the same roof as Lily — Mrs. Lily Shefford now. It was early — too early to get up and risk disturbing Dorothy. The clock on the dressing-table showed that it was barely half-past five.

Bertie lay gazing towards the window, remembering the week-end which was just past — August Bank Holiday week-end.

Saturday . . . The wedding . . .

Lily had kept her promise to have Dorothy and Nesta for bridesmaids, but the ceremony had been quite early in the morning and there had been little fuss. A simple meal in the church hall for about only eighteen guests — and then Dad had gone off with Lily for a short honeymoon. Bertie watched them go yet even then she could hardly believe that Dad would be returning with Lily as his wife.

Sunday . . . So very odd without her father . . .

Monday . . . And the knowledge that the honeymooners were returning that evening. She had put off till the last minute the making-up of the big double bed in the front bedroom, and when at last she began the task she could hear the excited voices of the children in the room below — all three of them eagerly waiting to welcome back Dad and Lily — oh, she would always be Lily to them all — yet, for all that, she *was* taking Mum's place . . . Her mother — it seemed to Bertie that she was the only one to remember. Even Dorothy, who had been quite big when Mrs. Shefford died, never mentioned Mum now . . .

Bertie had been still upstairs when the newly-weds arrived. She had heard all the excited voices below, and then Dad called, 'Bertie, Bertie — where are you?'

There had been presents for them all — a lovely brooch for herself with a long topaz drop. Dad had remembered that once she had said she would like a topaz — and this was a beauty. Pinned to the lapel of her blue suit it would look wonderful but . . .

She had forced herself to appear interested in Lily's description of

Devon, but inwardly she had felt miserable, especially after she had got to bed and in the next room could hear Dad's deep tones mingling with Lily's laughter . . . For the first time in a long while Bertie had cried.

Yet now, wakeful in the still house, she told herself she *ought* to be happy because *Dad* was so obviously happy.

She got up slightly before her usual time and went downstairs. She supposed they would have to come to some arrangement. Who was now to get breakfast, for instance?

Automatically Bertie began her regular morning chores. There was no sound from the big front bedroom upstairs. The children were all down before Dad appeared. Lily did not arrive till five minutes later and Bertie was just ready to dish up breakfast — haddock fillet with white sauce.

'Sorry!' Lily grinned rather sheepishly. 'I overslept. Now I'll have to get my skates on or I'll be late. Mustn't forget I'm still a working woman.'

Jack Shefford looked round at her as she slipped into a chair beside him. 'Don't bother coming this morning, Lil,' he said, and his tone was full of affection.

Bertie had come down very determined to be friends with Lily, telling herself they would have a talk and share out the home duties — that there was no reason why they shouldn't get on all right together. Yet now she could not help the surge of antipathy which went through her — just as it had that first time she heard her father say 'Lil' in a fond, adoring voice. She gritted her teeth. She would have to get used to hearing it, and she had better make up her mind to do it with a good grace.

She smiled as she said, 'An extra half-day off, Lily! Take it while you have the chance.'

The postman came just as Bertie was leaving. At least it had not been quite such a rush as usual, because Lily was going to wash up. 'Nothing for *me*, I suppose?' Bertie asked the question jokingly. The most she ever got addressed to her was a catalogue.

'Ah now — and there is something,' came the reply.

It was not an advertisement, either, which was thrust towards her. Bertie took the envelope and began to open it as she went along the path. There was a single sheet of notepaper inside, and she gave a gasp. This was from Bill . . .

'I am in Sotton — shall get into Scanlon station at 10.30 a.m. tomorrow (Tuesday). Please meet me but don't tell anyone — not *anyone*, mind, that I am home. I know you will not fail me.'

Bill home . . . and wanting *her* to meet him . . . What did it mean? She read the short note again before pushing it into her pocket.

When she got to White Farm she found Dud inside one of his glass-houses. 'Would you mind if I have part of the morning off? she asked, and then hastily explained, 'I want to go into Scanlon.'

'Of course — you go,' he replied.

'How's things?' he queried. 'Your Dad back all right?'

She nodded. At that moment the thought of Bill had overlaid any of her feelings about the situation at home.

The Sotton train was due in when Bertie reached the station. Bill . . . he was home again . . . in a few moments she would see him . . .

The engine came into sight and, with a noisy clanking, the carriages moved past her. Her eager glance scanned the windows. He had said he would be on this train, but she could not find him. Surely he would have been looking out — watching for her, as she was for him. A hand touched her arm from behind, and she whirled round. 'Bertie . . . '

She did not speak. How could she speak when she felt suddenly choked by the poignant emotions which ran through her with the swiftness of water down a mountain? This was Bill, but not the handsome young man who had been so good to look at. This man's face was scarred and disfigured. He said, 'You would not have known me if you had met me in the street.'

She swallowed that constricting lump in her throat.

'Wouldn't have *wanted* to know me maybe,' he said.

'Bill!' Indignation throbbed in that one word, and the expression in his eyes softened. 'Of course — you are Bertie. That's why I wanted to see you first. I knew you'd always be a friend — no matter what.'

He turned and began to move towards two suitcases on the platform. 'I'm going to put these in the left-luggage place,' he stated. 'Then we'll get outside.'

She watched him pick up his luggage. Tall, broad-shouldered, he looked just the same as he had been when she saw him move away from her to go on across the common . . . The same Bill, yet not the same . . .

When they were through the barrier and in the station yard Bertie glanced up at him. 'What — happened?' she asked.

'It was a tunnel accident. I suppose, really, I'm lucky to be alive but . . . oh, I can't talk about it. I want to go to Marcia but I'm scared — of what she will think of me — now that I'm like this. She . . . she never liked anything that wasn't pretty.' He spoke jerkily — he who had always been so sure of himself, had lost all his confidence.

He put a hand under her elbow. 'That is partly why I wanted you to come, Bertie. I just can't go and face her alone.'

His grip on her arm tightened. 'I want you to be with me.'

'But Bill . . . she is your wife . . . you've been away quite a long time. Surely . . .'

'No,' he broke in. Then, 'Please do this for me.'

'You mean you are going to Cordery straight away to see her?'

'Yes.'

'Are you being fair to Marcia?' Bertie

demanded. 'You ought to write to her — prepare her.'

'I must see the way she looks when I arrive.'

'But to go and confront her — just like that — when she doesn't even know you are in England. I tell you — it's not fair.'

'I confronted *you*, as you put it.'

'Bill, it's not the same . . .'

'Ah! You know Marcia too, don't you? Well, you can argue yourself blue in the face because you don't know Marcia — the way I do. I know this is something I have got to go through with, but I need support. *You* are not the sort to let a pal down.'

When they reached the bus stop the Cordery bus was waiting and within minutes they were off — along the road to the village. Bertie glanced several times at Bill's face as he gazed from the window. His lips were set. His expression showed no pleasure at sight of the familiar scene. So many times he had travelled this way on his motor-cycle.

So many times he had raced towards Cordery, eager to see Marcia . . .

Now he was going to find her — and he was so unsure of himself that he wanted Bertie's 'support'.

She felt distressed and miserably conscious that what he wanted was wrong. Marcia was his wife, as she had already told him, and they should be alone together when they met. It should have been Marcia who had gone to meet him . . .

But it had not been Marcia . . .

Once or twice Bertie opened her mouth to make a remark, and then decided to stay silent. What was there she could say when Bill was so quiet, so aloof?

They got off the bus and Bill moved towards the Fawleys' gate. Bertie lagged behind. Now that he was here he had forgotten her. He was remembering only that, beyond the well-known green door, was the woman he loved . . .

But Bertie was mistaken. Bill turned and looked back, halted. Slowly she went after him. 'Bill,' she began, but he interrupted, 'You go first. Don't let the gate click.'

She had always been prepared to do anything Bill asked her. She had always *wanted* to do things for him. She had loved looking after Rusty. But this was different. Yet though her heart rebelled against the thought of seeing Bill and Marcia meet, she still obeyed him. They approached the door quietly. In the small porch he whispered, 'You go on in. I'll be right behind you.'

And again she did what he ordered. She tapped on the door, turned the handle and called, 'Anyone home?'

It was Marcia's voice which answered, 'Come on in.' And Bertie almost sprinted along the narrow passage into the living-room. 'Marcia, you will never believe — it's Bill — he's here. He's . . . '

Bill spoke behind her then — just one word, 'Marcia.'

The girl across the room stood up, but she did not speak at all. Bertie had been determined to get out and leave the two together, but Bill was blocking the doorway. He moved one step towards Marcia, two steps . . .

Bertie saw the way the other girl's eyes dilated, how she put up her hand to her mouth — but most of all she was aware of the shrinking in Marcia's whole body. Bill spoke her name again, and it was as though the sound released a spring in Bertie so that she was able to move, meaning to slip out of the room behind him.

'No!' And that was the only word Marcia said to Bill, rejecting the hands he had suddenly reached towards her.

Abruptly Bill turned. He looked back over his shoulder, hesitated in the doorway. Then he was gone.

5

Bertie had seen the look in Bill's eyes as he turned away. Didn't Marcia see it too — that expression of utter hopelessness? Bertie said, 'He's your husband.'

When the other girl did not reply she asked fiercely, 'Don't you love him? Haven't you ever loved him?'

Still Marcia did not speak and Bertie added 'You're a monster if you won't stand by him now. You promised to 'keep him in sickness and health, for better or worse . . . ' '

And then Marcia said, 'I never made that vow.'

'You never promised . . . '

'You don't in a registry-office, you know.'

Suddenly Bertie moved. It was useless to try playing the advocate's part here. She must follow Bill — who had been so obviously hurt by his wife's attitude — even though it had not been unexpected by him. He had been afraid to face Marcia — afraid of the rejection in her eyes. Yet there must have been hope too in his heart, or he would not have come.

Now, with fear gripping her, Bertie ran down the Fawleys' path and out into the road. A man faced by utter despair might do anything . . .

She saw the bus coming, watched it halt at the stop on the corner for a solitary passenger to board it. Bill was gone and there was no other bus for half an hour. She hurried towards the corner. 'Oh, let someone come along and give me a lift . . . '

'Hard luck! Just missed it — guess you want to get to Scanlon, eh?'

Bertie glanced in gratitude at the man who had stopped and was opening the door of his van.

'Mike . . . Thanks.'

She tried to answer his remarks as they sped off. But she was concentrating on the road ahead, watching for the bus. They sighted it and Mike said, 'I don't expect we'll race it. I have to stop at a house just along here. You'll be in Scanlon, though, almost as soon as if you'd caught it.'

With frustration she saw the bus again disappear and Mike seemed to be gone ages, but when he came back he said, 'Now we're off. We'll overtake that bus yet.'

It was a game to him — he did not guess how desperately his passenger was willing him to win, had no idea how thwarted Bertie felt when she got no further glimpse of the large green vehicle in which Bill had rushed away from Cordery.

Mike said cheerfully, 'Well, here we are. Where would you like me to drop you?'

'Here, please,' she answered. They had reached the corner where the Cordery bus stopped to let off its passengers before going on to circle a block ready for its return to Cordery.

'Thank you, Mike — it was nice of you.'

But as soon as she was out of the van she had forgotten him — her only thought now was to find Bill. Surely he could not have gone far. She hurried along, her glance always ahead of her speeding feet as she searched for his tall figure among the folk on the pavements. Where would he be likely to go? Would he aim for any particular place — the station probably?

She reached the junction of two roads. The railway station was straight on . . . And in that moment she saw him. He was turning into a park — some little distance away to her left. She did not stop to walk. Her flying feet took her along the quiet road, in through the wide gateway.

She overtook him. 'Bill . . . ' She looked up at him, but he did not turn his head, did not even seem to know she was there. He plodded on and she kept pace with him, wondering what to say, what to do. She saw a bench just ahead of them. She put her hand on his arm. 'Bill, let's sit down for a minute.'

He obeyed her. She glanced at his face and then away. Such gloomy defeat in a face which had always been so gay, was terrible to see.

She held his arm with both her hands, and she spoke his name again, yearningly, 'Bill . . . '

'Bertie, I'm through.' The voice was filled with despair.

'No!' she asserted, her grip tightening.

'No? You saw the way she looked at me. I tell you I'm through.'

'Listen, Bill. Marcia was shocked when she saw you were altered — but you and she were in love, weren't you?'

'I was in love.'

'If you go back . . . ' Yet even as she spoke Bertie had a vision of Marcia — as she had been after Bill left. There had been no pity, even, in her eyes or voice.

Bill said, 'It's no use. I had to know — but I can't go back. I can never face

222

having her look at me as though . . . as though I'm some . . . dreadful horror.'

'Why didn't you write first and tell her — prepare her?'

'Because I hoped she was like you — inside. *You* didn't recoil.'

Oh Bill . . . Inside her now Bertie's emotions were like a flood-tide which threatened to tear down all her defences. She wanted to enfold him within the cocoon of her love. She wanted to fight for his happiness. Yet she could not even find words of comfort.

In a toneless voice he said, 'I'm on the scrap-heap. I might as well go and jump in the sea.'

'You won't feel that way tomorrow.' Now Bertie had found words. Suddenly, beating all through her, was the assurance — nobody else needed her anymore — but Bill did. Bill!

She said, 'I'll look after you.' He was down and out — broken, but she would stand by him. 'Come on — I have a plan.'

As she stood up her hand under his arm was firm, and he did not resist her. He went with her when she made her way to the railway station where he had left his luggage. He had been prepared for Marcia's rejection, but not prepared for afterwards.

She said, 'I bet you haven't had anything to eat for ages,' and propelled him into the station hotel. She was not used to hotels but there was a door marked 'Lounge', and into this she marched. Bill followed. He seemed to have no will of his own. He might have been a docile child, obeying a mother's mandates without question. She pointed to an armchair.

'You stay there a minute or two — I'll be back,' she said. Then she went in search of someone in charge. She met a man in the passage, and assuming what she hoped was an air of authority, she said, 'My friend — he is in the lounge — in the chair behind the door — he is unwell. Will you provide him with dinner and let him stay here till I get back?'

She paused, opening her handbag before she added, 'I expect I'll be an hour or two. I could pay you something now . . . '

'No, no — it's quite all right, Miss.' She saw his glance go to her left hand and wished she had said brother instead of friend. 'We'll look after the gentleman till you return.'

'Thank you.' In the lounge again, she said to Bill, 'Promise you'll wait here for me.'

He did not look up at her or answer and she put a hand on his shoulder. 'Bill, promise,' she urged. He nodded apathetically then and she said briskly, 'I'll not be a minute longer than I can help. Bill, I'm coming back to you as soon as I can.' Again he nodded.

She managed to get a bus returning to Cordery after a wait of only a few moments. Going indoors she found Lily in the kitchen. She was at the table, hands floury, in the process of preparing a meal. She looked up as Bertie went in.

'How have you ever managed to work in this place for so long?' Lily demanded. 'The table is in the darkest corner of the room, isn't it? We'll have a few alterations made. I can't see why we can't have a bigger window. The cooker wants moving over there and . . . '

In the kitchen which for so long had been Bertie's own domain . . . Lily was already planning some of her famous alterations.

Yet now Bertie felt no irritation — nothing at all. Suddenly it did not matter what Lily did.

'Don't you think my ideas are good?'

'Yes, yes, I suppose so. But it would never work, Lily — you and me here together. I've got the unexpected chance of a job — away — and I'm going to take it.'

'Because you don't like me coming here?'

'Won't you *really* be glad if I go? Lily, there is no need to deny it.'

'Bertie, you can't do this. How about . . . '

'I don't mind 'how about' anything, Lily. You can all get on very well without me.' Bertie ran upstairs and pushed things hastily into a couple of suitcases — one large, the other small. A good thing they had not been returned to the loft after the honeymoon. She put into her handbag the last week's wages she had received from Dud, and her post office savings bank book. There was not much in it but it might be useful.

She went to the bathroom and took a small phial of tablets from the bathroom cabinet there. Then she sat down and wrote two hurried notes — the first to her father, the other to Dud. She hoped she would not be letting Dud down — but he had Eve now and she knew more about farming than Bertie did.

She picked up the suitcases and went down the stairs. She wanted to be away from the house before her father got home.

She did not want to see the hurt that would inevitably spring into Dad's eyes if he thought his marriage was driving her away from home. Yet she had spoken the truth when she said it wouldn't work — with herself and Lily in the same house. For too long Bertie had been sole mistress here and, even if Bill had not turned up like this, she could not have stayed home. But that she was going with Bill, she would admit to no one.

Bertie reached the front door. She expected Lily to appear but everything was very quiet — too quiet for anyone except herself to be in the place . . .

Putting down her cases, she ran hastily through to the kitchen. It was empty and the back door wide open. Lily had realised Bertie was packing up and gone racing off to Dad — to her husband.

Swift compunction seared Bertie's heart. She hated the thought that she might be giving her father worry — but after all it would be only a passing worry — and better than a gradual realisation of disagreement between his daughter and new wife.

Hastily she unfolded the letter she intended to leave for him. On the bottom of it she scribbled, 'All my love, Dad. I'll never forget your goodness to me. I do want you to be happy — you and Lil, too. It is only fair to you both that you have a chance to begin your new life together without any sort of frustration . . . '

Abruptly she stopped. That was not exactly what she had wanted to say when she so impulsively began that postscript. But it would have to do.

She left the note on the table and as she ran back along the hall she was whispering tensely, 'Be happy, Dad — you must be happy.'

Picking up her cases, she hurried away from the house. Vividly the sight of the lobelia and alyssum along the border etched itself on her memory.

Often she had managed to get lifts to

Scanlon when she needed them, but today she did not intend to rely on chance. Besides, she had luggage. She turned unwaveringly to the left. Now Mike was to have her as a customer — if he was in. Oh, he *must* be home . . . back from his recent trip into the town.

Mike was obviously surprised to see her but she had her explanation ready. 'Yes, she had made a sudden decision to take a job away — it was a chance you couldn't afford to miss when it came. No, she hadn't ever had the chance before to find out what the world beyond Scanlon was like. Yes, she was excited. No, she wasn't afraid of being alone and away from her friends . . . '

All the way to Scanlon she answered his questions. It was a big step, she agreed. What she did not tell him was that she was doing it for Bill.

She was glad when they reached the station. Mike carried her cases to the ticket office and put them down.

Turning away, he said, 'Good luck, Bertie.' Then he grinned, 'Though I don't know whether I need wish you that. *You* will fall on your feet all right.'

She watched the young man go. *If only you knew what my job is, you'd think I needed luck . . .*

Stooping, she picked up her cases and put them in a corner. Then she began to make her way to the Station Hotel. It was not till she reached the door that sudden fear gripped her heart. Bill had looked dazed but, underneath, his mind had been concerned with only one fact — that Marcia had rejected him. And that fact had destroyed his will to live. 'I might as well jump in the sea . . . ' Suppose, *suppose* he had gone — and she did not know where to look . . .

But he was still there — still in the lounge, though in a different chair. A middle-aged man sat beside him, talking in a loud voice but apparently needing only a listener, for Bill was not answering and he quite obviously did not see Bertie when she looked in at him.

As she stood rather uncertainly in the doorway a voice spoke behind her. 'Ah, there you are, Miss.' She turned to face the man she had seen before.

'Your friend has had dinner, like you asked. He seems a bit far-away. Has he had some sort of a shock?'

'Yes, yes,' she agreed quickly. 'Thank you for looking after him. Now, how much do I owe you?'

The sum he mentioned was larger than she had expected but she paid it without comment. Then she made her way to Bill. He still appeared stunned. When she spoke his name he looked up at her.

'Come along,' she said in a firm voice, and without hesitation he stood up, following her out of the hotel and into the station booking office. She bought tickets to Waterloo.

'Next train due in ten minutes,' she was told by the man who clipped her ticket. She was moving with fixed determination, though she had no real plan. All she knew was that Bill was in the depths of despair — that *she* was the one he had sent for. She was his life-line and she must see that her anchorage was firm.

She bought a newspaper and then, remembering that she herself had had no dinner, procured a packet of sandwiches from the buffet.

The train came in and Bill went with her into a second class compartment. To her relief, they were off almost at once. Back of her mind had been the fear that her father might follow her when he got from Lily the news of Bertie's flight.

Bill was in the corner seat and after they had travelled some distance she tried to talk to him — but to all her remarks he answered simply yes or no. She offered him the newspaper and he took it. Yet though he made a pretence of reading it, she knew he was not giving any attention to the news.

She ate her sandwiches and then

leaned back in her seat, closing her eyes. She was trying to see a way ahead of her. When she got to London what would she do? But surely it would be easy enough to find a couple of rooms — one for Bill first. She would have to see him settled in — and she must not be too far away from him for a while. It was imperative that she should keep an eye on him until he roused out of his lethargy and made up his mind that, though he might not be able to have Marcia now, life *was* still worth living.

Her hand was on the seat beside her and all at once she found Bill's closing over it — clinging to it. She glanced round at him, but he was gazing away through the window. He must have felt her move yet he did not look at her. She wished she could see the expression in his eyes now. Was he conscious of the checkered landscape beyond that window — or so introvertly aware still of Marcia and her rejection of him that nothing outside could impinge on his mind or feelings?

He held her hand during the whole of the journey, as though the touch of her gave him a certain measure of security or comfort. As they neared the smoke-blackened outskirts of London she said, 'Bill, do you know any place where you could stay?'

'No. Does it matter much?'

'Of course it matters,' she retorted, 'but I don't know if it will be easy to find anywhere.' London was such an unknown quantity to her — unknown and rather frightening.

So it was, perhaps, natural that she should try the first place she came to — a grimy-looking house that had a rather dirty card in the window announcing 'Bed and Breakfast'.

Bill stood on the pavement with their luggage while she went up two steps to knock on a door which was opened by an old woman.

'Two single rooms?' She repeated Bertie's request and shook her head. 'One double, that's all,' she replied.

Bertie hesitated. Then she said, 'Well,

I'll take the double one for my brother.' She said the last word without any hesitation. 'Then I'll go and find a room for myself somewhere else. Perhaps I can bring my own luggage in — just temporarily?'

'I don't care what the blinking hell you do as long as I gets me dough,' came the quick retort. 'And before you comes in I'll have me deposit too. I bin had before today as ever was.' As a dirty hand was thrust towards her Bertie felt a surge of repulsion. It would be impossible to leave Bill here. Turning away, she marched down the steps.

'Come on,' she said to Bill. But she did not have much better luck at any other place. Perhaps because it was near the station she saw time after time the two words, 'No Vacancies'. Then at last a door was opened to her by a woman wearing a clean apron.

'Sorry — I've only got one room,' Bertie was told, 'and I'd like a deposit.' They were a suspicious lot round here, but at least the request now had been made with a smile. Opening her purse, Bertie handed over a pound note. She said, 'My brother will stay here. Perhaps you know a place where I could get a room close by for myself?'

The woman was leading the way along a passage and up some narrow stairs. She said, 'Try two doors along — she might take you in there.'

They reached a landing and a door was flung open. 'There — it's comfortable — make yourselves at home.'

As she stepped into the room Bertie gave an involuntary shudder.

This place had looked not too bad from outside and the woman's clean apron had been misleading. But she had paid now — and Bill did not seem to care about the grubbiness and lack of comfort.

She looked round as she said slowly, 'We'll leave our things here and go out to get a meal of some sort . . . '

'No, no . . . I don't want to go out again.' But Bertie was suddenly conscious that she was very hungry. Except for those couple of sandwiches in the train she had had nothing since breakfast.

'All right,' she said, 'then I'll go out and get something.'

'Bertie . . . ' He looked up with the first evidence of interest since she had found him in Scanlon. 'You won't be long? You'll — come back . . . '

'Of course I'll be back,' she told him quickly. 'But at the moment I'm starving.'

On the first corner she came to was a fish and chip shop, and without hesitation she went in. When she got back with her newspaper-wrapped parcel and a bottle of Tizer, Bill was standing by the window.

'Come on,' she ordered. 'This isn't a very big table — and we don't have any plates or knives and forks, but we'll manage.'

Bill had most of the Tizer but he ate very little of the fish and chips she gave him. She wrapped all the remains together and, standing up, said, 'I'll take this away with me. I've got to go now and find a room for myself.'

His eyes as he glanced at her were full of panic — so different all at once from the state of apathy which had held him ever since he left Marcia in the Fawley's kitchen.

'Bill, I'll find somewhere close,' she assured him. 'Tomorrow we must search for something else, but for tonight you will have to put up with this and I must find a room of some kind. You get to bed and have a sleep. I'll be back in the morning.'

'No! Don't leave me. I'm all right as long as you are here. Just now I began to think you would *not* come back — and it was awful. If you go I think I'll die. I can't face it — not now I'm back and things are so different from what I hoped. Coming home on the boat and wanting to believe what happened to me could make no difference to — her . . . Going down in the train . . . and still hoping and now . . . '

He was like a child afraid of being left

in the dark — only *he* was not a child, and *he* was afraid of his thoughts — seared by an experience which might drive him to do — what?

'I might as well go and jump in the sea . . .'

Involuntarily Bertie's glance went to the fireplace with its inevitable slot-meter gas fire.

She moved towards him and suddenly he was clinging to her. 'Bertie, don't leave me,' he begged. 'I can't face the night alone. You brought me here. You can't desert me — now.'

She did not know what to reply, but at last into the silence she said, 'All right.' Her tone was level — matter-of-fact. 'I reckon you are about all-in.' Her arms were around him. He would never know what an effort it cost her to sound normal. 'You will feel better tomorrow. I'm going to give you some aspirins — they will make you sleep.'

Bill needed release from his despairing thoughts, and the tablets she had in her bag were more potent than aspirin.

Deliberately she had brought them from the medicine cabinet at home — sleeping-pills prescribed for her father a little while ago when he had neuralgia.

She turned but still Bill held her. 'Bertie, you won't sneak out on me directly I'm asleep? If you don't promise me that I'll not take the aspirin.' It was almost as though he had been able to read what was in her mind. How *could* she stay here all night? What would the landlady say if she knew?

Oh, bust the landlady — bust propriety! Nothing mattered except Bill. 'No, I'll look after you,' she said. 'That's a promise.'

'You'll stay?'

'Yes.'

He was docile again then. She said, 'I'm going to dump this fish and chip paper in a bin outside in the road. Then I'll wash my hands — there's a bathroom of sorts just along the passage. You get into bed while I'm gone.'

* ★ ★

An hour later she was sitting in a chair by the window, listening to Bill's regular breathing which was interspersed at intervals with a deep in-drawn sigh which sounded almost like a sob. Bertie's hands, clenched together in her lap, tightened involuntarily every time it happened.

It got dark but a street lamp threw a narrow beam right across the room. By its light she presently got up and went towards the bed. Bill was an indistinct hump beneath the bedclothes, but his head was dark on the pillow. He was turned away from her.

For a while she stood looking down at him. She thought, I can't sit up all night on that small hard chair . . . Slowly, inch by inch, she eased herself on to the bed.

Not till she was lying down did she realise how tired she was. All at once the whole of her body was throbbing. She had never felt like this since the day she rushed off to Sotton — the day Bill emigrated. That had been her first realisation of the fact that emotion could be far more wearing than hard work.

6

When she woke it was light and Bill, on one elbow, was looking down at her. As her eyes opened and she met his gaze a thrill of unbelief went through her. Then she remembered, and abruptly she sat up. She said, 'Hullo.' Then matter-of-factly, 'I'll go and see if I can get us a cup of tea.'

'Where do you imagine you can go to do that?'

'The station, I shouldn't be surprised. Surely I ought to be able to get some — in those cardboard cup things. I've seen people get them from a machine in Scanlon, so surely they'd have them in London.'

'Knowing you, I shouldn't wonder if you do get some,' he answered, and swept a hand over his hair. 'I could use a cup of tea. I have the grandfather of all headaches this morning.'

Yet if he felt unwell, he sounded more cheerful. She slipped off the bed and went quickly across to the door. 'I'll do my best, anyway,' she told him.

She crept quietly along the passage and down the stairs. She wondered what would happen if she were discovered sneaking out.

As she neared the front door she was afraid she would find it locked, but it opened to her turn of the handle — and she was outside. It was early yet already there was hustle and bustle in the streets and a lack of that deliciously fresh tang of a morning in Cordery. She had a swift nostalgic memory of the common and Rusty and Joe . . .

She could not find tea, but she procured coffee, and from the station buffet buttered rolls and hard boiled eggs.

Bill was up when she got back, and rather silently they had their impromptu breakfast. The coffee was muddy-looking and, as she sipped it, Bertie said, 'It's not very nice.'

'It was all right,' he replied. He had drunk his in one gulp as soon as she got in.

When they had finished she looked across at him. She said, 'You need a shave and I want a wash. I'll go back to the station and into the cloakroom there. Then I'm going to look for somewhere to stay. Very certain it is that I must find somewhere better than this.'

He stood up, moved round the table. His hands as he reached them towards her were trembling. Getting to her feet, she said, 'Bill, you must be sensible. We have got to work out some plan . . .'

He was so big and she had thought him so strong. Inwardly she felt an aching hurt that *he* could be vulnerable to what had happened to him. 'Bill, it's not the end of the world. You have got to help me to help you . . .'

He gripped her shoulders. 'You love me, don't you?' he demanded, but she did not answer.

He said slowly, 'I saw it in your eyes when you woke up and looked at me this morning. No, I knew it before — when I realised you were on the bed beside me. No woman would do for a man what you did yesterday and last night — unless she loved him.'

Still she was silent. She did not look up at him. Her eyes were on a level with his neck. She could see a pulse beating in his throat. Her own heart thudded.

'Bertie . . . ' She felt the sudden tightening of his hands on her shoulders, and even before he spoke she knew what he was asking her to do. His voice lacked any sort of expression. 'Bertie — you and I — couldn't we make a go of it?'

She raised her glance to his face. Wasn't he offering what she had always wanted - - himself? She said falteringly, 'I . . . I . . . Yes, I do love you, Bill. I always have . . . ever since that first day when I met you with Rusty on the common. But when I came away with you I . . . I didn't mean it to be . . . that way. I just wanted to help you . . . to be near you.'

'Like a sister, eh? Well . . . Ever since I went away I've been alone — I wanted it that way but now — I can't go on any longer. What sort of plans can I make — for myself? There's no point . . . '

His hands dropped from her and she saw his eyes as he turned away. She caught at his arm. 'Bill, oh Bill . . . My dear . . . '

She had never believed she would have the right to call him that — yet now he had given her that right. She stood in front of him and, reaching up, put her hands one on each side of his head. She drew his face down to her level, and deliberately she kissed that ugly scar on his cheek.

Suddenly his arms were round her. He buried his face in her neck.

* * *

'We *can't* stay here,' Bertie said. It was later that morning. She was sitting in the chair by the window. Bill was lying on the bed. He might not have heard her remark. He had accepted the fact that she was prepared to stay with him. Now he seemed to have lost interest again in everything. They would have to eat — even though he appeared not to worry about it. Besides, she had no right to be staying in this room — even if she wanted to, which she did not.

'Surely it must be possible to find a room or two that would be clean and comfortable.' She spoke her thoughts aloud, but Bill did not reply. As she stood up she looked across at him. He had not told her just how badly he had been injured — nor how long he had been in hospital. It could be that he was still suffering from the effects of the accident which had scarred his face. But she would bring him back to health and happiness — of that she was determined. In the meantime, till he could do some work, she would have to find a job herself. If they were to live they must have money — and that Bill had not mentioned.

Slowly she moved towards the door.

The knob was loose and rattled as she turned it. Quickly Bill looked up. 'Bertie, you won't be long . . . ' His eyes held the panic which came every time he thought she was going to leave him alone.

For a long moment she stood gazing across at him. 'You love me', he had said. He knew it and was prepared to take her for granted because of it. Well, she did love him, and at the moment that meant she must mother him too . . .

She said patiently, 'I don't believe you heard what I said a moment ago. I must go out and get something for us to eat and some different place to stay . . . '

She moved a step or two back towards him.

'Bill, come with me . . . '

'No, no.'

She realised it would be useless to argue — he was determined to stay indoors. She turned quickly. This time she did not pause nor glance back.

She had not mentioned her intention of trying to get some work, though she felt that must be her first objective. But how to start? What qualifications had she to offer — she who had never had a job except the one at White Farm?

She walked slowly, aimlessly along until she reached a shop where she had bought some fruit during the morning and where the woman had appeared very friendly. At the moment she was busy, chatting and joking with several customers who crowded round the open front of her greengrocery store. Bertie waited till the women had all gone. Then hastily she approached the shop-keeper.

'I'm wondering if you can help me,' Bertie began. 'I'm looking for a job . . . ' She hesitated, faltered to a stop. She was not used to asking for favours.

'What kind of job, like?'

'I don't know. I'd do anything to tide me over while I look round . . . ' Bertie was aware of the sudden quick appraisal

251

of brown shrewd eyes. 'You come from the country, eh, my girl?'

'Well . . . yes . . . '

'What did you do there?'

'Oh . . . looked after the family . . . worked on a farm.'

'Then, finding it dull, ran away to look for your fortune in London, eh?'

Bertie did not reply and the woman chuckled. 'I've seen other girls do just the same — but fortunes aren't any more easy to pick up in the city — as you'll find.' Two customers approached and she added, 'Wait a minute or two.'

More folk arrived to buy fruit and vegetables. When they had gone the woman turned back to Bertie. 'How about references?' she asked.

'Well, yes . . . ' She could give Dud's name. 'Where I worked on the farm . . . '

'That's O.K. Can you count?'

'Oh yes!'

'Then I could use you here — temporary-like.'

'Here!'

'Don't sound so surprised. You said you was looking, and my nipper has just taken herself off to work in a gown shop. If she comes back you'd have to go — understood?' The woman gave a chuckle again. 'You helped grow things — now you can sell 'em. When can you start?'

'Tomorrow? I want to look round for somewhere to live today.'

'Like what did you have in mind?'

'A flat if I can get it.'

'That's a tall order! You can't know how hard it is to get 'em.'

'Oh dear . . . '

'I tell you what — there's three rooms above this — used to live there myself — always meant to let them to anyone that came to work for me. Because I knew I'd have to get someone if the nipper left me. You're in luck coming along just now before I've had the energy to find anyone else.'

'Oh yes — I am lucky,' Bertie agreed. 'Can I look at the rooms?'

'Help yourself — through the door at

the back there and up the steps — two floors up — first one's my store.' She pointed. 'Key's on the hook there — the furthest one in . . . ' The woman stood back to let Bertie pass her. She added, 'And my name's South — what's yours?'

Bertie told her and then said, 'Thank you for trusting me.'

'Oh, Minnie South can usually pick 'em out, my dear. I've never been let down yet — I don't think you will do it, either.'

★   ★   ★

Two nights later Bertie wrote home. She told them she was happy, that she had found a 'nice flat' and was working in a florist's shop. But she did not mention Bill — and at the head of the paper was an accommodation address.

As she sealed the envelope she told herself she was happy — she was with Bill and that must be for her the acme of contentment. Yet during the weeks

254

which followed she was often filled with depression. Bill had wanted the comfort of her nearness but, for her, there was only loneliness. Most of the time he was silent and so aloof that he might almost just as well have been still in New Zealand.

In the first moment of her surrender to him — that morning after their arrival in London — she had thought that her own fierce loving would be sufficient. Yet *now* she felt an even greater frustration than in those days back in Cordery when she had loved without hope. *Now* she wanted the whole of him — and she would fight for what she wanted so desperately. Time after time she banished her oppression by telling herself — One day he will learn to love me — I'll *make* him really love me.

Regularly she wrote a letter home and one evening as she finished her task she glanced up to the realisation that Bill was watching her.

She licked the flap of the envelope

and pressed it firmly down.

'You never show me what you write,' Bill said slowly. 'You won't let them know where I am.'

She got up from her seat at the table and went to sit beside him on an old leather settle. 'Let's have this out,' she said. 'Suppose — Marcia wants to find you?'

'She won't. *You* know how she hated anything unpleasant. I had to see her — to find out how she felt about me — like I am now . . . '

'But you didn't give her much chance to . . . '

'Get over the shock of seeing me?' he put in. 'She'll never do that. Marcia loved my face because it was handsome.' He spoke without any shade of pride — he was stating a fact. He had known he was good-looking. Bertie said, 'First of all she fell in love with your face. Surely — afterwards it was you . . . '

'As long as I was still good to look at.'

'You don't know that. She has had

time to think about it now.'

'I don't want her pity.'

'But Bill . . . '

Suddenly he put his hand on her arm. His grip was hard enough to hurt.

He asked, 'Are you tired of me — already? Are you trying to tell me that?'

'No!'

'Then listen. For me Marcia is something I have written off — we won't ever talk about her. From now on it's me and you. Agreed?'

'Yes . . . Oh, Bill . . . '

He was nodding towards the letter she had left on the table. 'What have you told them?'

'Not much. They think I am alone of course.'

'Would you be *ashamed* to admit you were living with me?'

'Bill, you didn't want me to tell them . . . '

He put his arm round her and pulled her against him. His voice was husky as he said, 'You're a good little pal,

257

Bertie — and what a selfish brute I am — thinking about *me* all the time.' He put his cheek against hers. 'No regrets?'

'Of course not, Bill.'

'And you still love me — despite all my egotism and ill-humour?'

'More than ever now,' she declared.

'Then show me.' He leaned his head back. 'Push your fingers through my hair — kiss me — you don't need to be taught how to make love, do you?'

For a moment she sat looking at him. He was very still. His eyes were closed.

The incredible — the impossible had happened. Through all the years she had loved Bill — worshipped him silently from afar. She had seen him fall in love with Marcia — known searing jealousy at thought of his possession of the other girl's loveliness. She had felt utterly desolate when she saw him go away on a ship that would take him thousands of miles from her. Yet now he was back — and he was saying — 'Show me that you love me.' He was saying it to plain Bertie Shefford — who had so often amused him . . .

★ ★ ★

But he did not find their life together amusing. He needed her — and that gave her a great deal of satisfaction. As the days slipped by she knew she was beginning to win her fight against the apathy which had drained him of energy and made him apparently scared of going out. She persuaded him to go with her sometimes on a bus to a near-by park. That was the start to a campaign of coaxing and pushing which resulted at last in the triumph of seeing him apply for a job — which he obtained.

They settled into a placid routine and Bertie was happily content that when he returned from work each day Bill needed no diversion outside their small flat.

They had no neighbours. The entry to their home was in a cul-de-sac at the back of Mrs. South's shop. All the other premises were used as storehouses, so they were isolated in their own small haven, and no one except themselves ever mounted the outside iron stairway to their door.

Sometimes Bertie wondered half-guiltily what they would all think at home if they could see the flowers in the 'florist's' shop which she wrote about in her letters. Partly-withered bunches of daisies and marigolds were pushed unartistically in earthenware jars above the stacks of fruit. Often she felt homesick for the garden at Cordery and many times she remembered that last glimpse of it — the blue and white flowers which she had planted so light-heartedly in the spring . . . That was before she knew anything about Lily and Dad — or that Bill would come back . . .

Bill . . . He was the only thing in her life that mattered now. Bill — *her* Bill. *She* did not see that dreadful scar, though she knew that *he* never forgot it

— just as she knew he had not forgotten Marcia. 'We won't ever talk about her,' he had said, and so she had done as he wished, hoping that one day she would come to know that her own image had ousted Marcia's.

But how long would that take?

Weeks became a couple of months, but she knew that even in his arms at night she was only a woman. She knew that the Bill who had made love to her was not a man in love. He was too easily satisfied. When she wanted to cling to him he was gently resistant. Soon — too soon he had remembered that Marcia was far away. Her name might not be mentioned but she was never really banished from between them. And so, after Bill was asleep, Bertie would lie awake beside him, hands clenched, wild emotions churning inside her.

Bill I love you so much, so much . . . Please love me . . . really love me . . . Desperately she tried to get her message through to his sleeping mind.

They said that telepathy was possible. If only she wished hard enough she could get right inside his thoughts . . .

But at least he seemed content. They might have been married for ages she thought sometimes when she put their meals on the table, or ironed his shirts while he sat by the gas-fire reading his newspaper. The time she liked best of all was the half-hour before bed-time when they sat on the old settle, and Bill talked — often about his life in New Zealand. But it did not matter what he said. During that brief time Bertie was happier than ever in her life. Bill's arm was round her and he was chattering away to her — relaxed and cheerful. Surely he, too, was happy . . .

It was one evening in October when Bill did not come home at his usual time. This was something that had never happened before. Bertie had his dinner ready. Well, it would not spoil for half an hour, she told herself. He must have been delayed in some way, and at any minute he would be here . . .

But he failed to arrive. She did not even think of having her own meal. Every second she expected to hear the sound of his hand on the door latch — the low whistle which was his regular greeting to her.

She tried to ignore her rising anxiety but at last, after more than an hour of waiting, she could not stem her panic. She did not wait to put on a coat. She did not remember that outside there was a biting wind. She ran hastily down the steps to the pavement and flew along to the phone box on the corner. Then, lifting the telephone receiver, she paused, put it down again and began to search through the directory for the name of Bill's firm.

At last she got through. She could hear the burr of the bell that was ringing at the other end — ringing, ringing — forcing her to admit to herself at last that the building must surely be empty. Which meant that Bill must have left work. Where was he now? Something had happened to keep him from coming home.

With trembling fingers she dialled again. The police — they would know if there had been an accident . . .

'Yes, yes,' she said, when a voice answered her. 'It's my husband — he's late. No — he never *is* late. I think he may have had an accident.' In reply to a couple of questions she gave Bill's name and where he worked. Then she said, 'Yes, yes, I will . . . ' That remote voice had told her to 'hang on' while enquiries were made.

As she waited she seemed able to see the cynical expression which must have matched the voice after her statement that Bill was late. They *expected* husbands to be often late. They did not know hers . . .

Bertie bit hard on her lip. So glibly she had said, 'My husband.' Yet he was *not* that. Suppose . . . But Bill would never walk out on her . . . How could she ever let the thought cross her mind?

'Yes,' she said quickly into the

telephone, 'yes, I'm still here.' She listened while the voice said unemotionally that a man *had* been admitted to hospital. 'No, I don't suppose he would have anything in his pocket to identify him. He didn't carry any papers or anything with him,' she said. 'Yes, of course I'll come,' she added when it was suggested she should go along to the hospital to see if it was Bill.

She *knew* — in her heart she knew that the man in the hospital bed was Bill — and he was unconscious, not able to tell them who he was. He might be dying . . .

She had to go home to fetch her handbag but still she gave no thought to the need for a coat. It could have been only minutes before she stood at his side. She whispered, 'Bill, I'm here . . . ' But he did not stir and the sister, behind her, said quietly, 'He has concussion but we don't think he is too badly hurt. Perhaps you will tell me your husband's name — and your address . . . telephone number . . . '

'That means you think there is danger . . . '

'No, no,' the sister interrupted as Bertie hesitated. 'It is just the usual procedure to ask.'

'I can give you the number of the shop where I work during the day,' Bertie said, 'but at night that would be no use. I must stay here tonight. I must be near him.'

'No, you go home and try not to worry,' the other woman replied. 'I promise we will let you know if you are needed.'

'How could you do that?'

'The police could contact you within minutes,' smiled the sister, 'but I assure you that your husband is going to be all right. If you come in tomorrow I am convinced he will know you then.'

Bill was not in hospital many days but, after a visit the morning following his admission, Bertie was unable to go in to see him again. Certainly she had been out in a bitter wind minus a coat, but so she had been many times in Cordery. Perhaps London air affected her differently. In any case she developed a terrible cold which she felt it would be impossible to take into a hospital ward.

When Bill returned he was very quiet and she wondered if he was blaming her for not going to see him. She said at last, 'I'm sorry — I felt pretty groggy.'

'You look a bit queer now,' he retorted. 'Get off to bed and don't worry about me.'

And she went. Weakly she was near to tears. Had he meant to sound bitter when he said those last words? 'Don't worry about me ... ' as though implying that had been her attitude while he was in hospital.

But she thought she knew him well enough to believe he would not nurse a grievance for long. And surely he must realise her cold was genuine. Yet the next day he was still withdrawn and aloof — reminding her of those first days in London.

At length she could stand it no more and demanded, 'Bill, what's the matter? If I've done something to upset you . . . '

'No, you haven't,' he answered quickly. 'Come and sit down.'

She went to him, and there was an odd sense of foreboding in her heart. Suppose he was going to tell her there was someone else? But as soon as she was settled at his side his arm went round her.

'Bertie — the doctor in hospital suggested I should have an operation.'

'Oh! What for? Bill, when that car knocked you down you were more badly hurt than you told me . . . '

'No, no. An operation on my — scar,' he said.

'He says they can — they can — take it away?'

'Well, make it hardly noticeable maybe.'

'Then of course you must have it done,' she told him.

'Can I face it?' he replied slowly.

'Hoping it would be gone, and then perhaps finding their miracle did not really work?'

'It would be worth trying,' she insisted. 'Didn't you agree at once?'

'No, I said I'd let him know.'

Almost he seemed scared at the idea of the plastic surgery which would be necessary, and for days he did not make up his mind. Then one evening he came in and announced, 'I went to the hospital this afternoon. It means I'll have to go away. They'll send for me when they can do it.'

'Christmas is getting near,' she said. 'You won't be away then?'

He did not answer at once and she asked, 'Bill, you don't *want* to be away?'

'I was thinking about you,' he told her. 'You had a letter from home, didn't you, and they suggested you should go back for the holiday. Won't they think it odd if you don't?'

'Why would they? Bill, we could have a lovely time — turkey and Christmas pudding and all . . . '

He put his cheek against hers — it was a familiar gesture now. She rubbed her own face up and down against his. 'Dear little Bertie,' he said. 'Of course, we'll have our Christmas together. Can't you imagine how lost I'd be without you?'

'Oh, Bill . . . ' Could he possibly know how happy those words had made her?

They had a wonderful time. When the evening of Boxing Day came Bertie felt she had had a taste of heaven.

For the first time she had been able to forget Marcia completely. Because *he* had too?

But it was all too brief. The New Year brought a message that Bill was to go almost immediately for his operation.

She said despondently, 'You'll be miles away. I won't be able to see you.'

'No — pity the place is so far.' The special surgeon operated only at his own hospital. 'Anyway,' Bill added, 'I'll write — and I'll be back with you before any time.'

On the day he left he leaned out of the train window, waving till he was carried round a bend and out of sight. But for long moments Bertie stood where she was. The desolation in her heart matched that of the time when she had seen him sail for New Zealand.

As at last she turned away she gave herself a shake, determining to fill her time by giving the flat a thorough cleaning. She could put on some paint — paper the rooms in something bright. If she crammed every spare minute with work the time might go more quickly.

But the evenings were inevitably lonely — and it seemed pointless to cook for herself. So she lived mostly on bread-and-butter, cheese, cold meat and fruit.

Bill wrote that he was to have a pedicle graft and added, 'Keep your fingers crossed.' After that she did not hear for nearly a week, though she wrote every day herself.

When she heard he was coming home she looked eagerly round at the results of her labours — she had transformed their little nest.

Now to lay in supplies. She could not cook a meal because she must go to meet him — but she laid the table and made all the other preparations so that when they got back she had only to put on a kettle.

Then she donned the new coat she had managed to buy and sped off to catch a bus to the station. It was a long train and she watched the carriages sliding past her without a glimpse of the face she loved. With a series of clangs the train stopped. Still she could not see Bill.

Suddenly hands were put on her shoulders from behind. It had happened like this on the day she met him when he returned from abroad. But this time it was he who swung her round to face him. 'Well, how do you like me?' he asked, and she could hear the excitement in his voice.

For a moment she gazed up at him. Where that ugly scar had been was now no more than a thin, hardly perceptible thread of white. 'Well?' he demanded again, and she felt a contraction of her heart.

'Bill, I'd like you — any way,' she said quietly.

'Come on.' He took her arm and began to propel her toward the barrier. 'My girl, we are going to celebrate,' he announced.

'But I've got a meal all ready at home,' she protested, 'your favourite — salmon salad.'

'Oh, bust that!' he exclaimed and did not guess how his exclamation hurt her. He could not realise how difficult and expensive it had been to get salad at this time of the year — that the effort and money had been an expression of her love . . .

He was adding, 'Come along, I'm going to take you somewhere really posh.' He put his arm round her, hugging her close against his side. He was smiling, gay, and his mood was infectious. She said, 'Nowhere less posh than the Ritz!'

But inwardly she was longing for the moment when they would be home — where he could hug her and kiss her properly . . .

7

Bill followed her up the stairs and, inside the door of their living-room, she stopped. They had been separated for several weeks — the letters he had written were scrappy and unsatisfying. She was hungry for the feel of his arms round her and disappointed when he did not immediately reach for her but stood looking round, an expression on his face that was unfamiliar to her. If he was noting her decorations he was not *pleased* with them. She asked quietly, 'Aren't you glad to be home?'

'Yes.' His reply came quickly but she was very aware of his pause before he added, 'Of course.'

'Bill . . . ' The uncertainty in her voice made him look down at her and he said, 'It's so small after the largeness of the hospital.'

'When we first came here you said it

was cosy — being small.'

'Did I? More likely you said it and I agreed!'

He could remember that time and how it had been — with himself having no opinion or will of his own.

And then he stooped to kiss her, but the thrill she had anticipated was missing. She had been wanting him so desperately. *He* had not been so anxious to get back to *her*.

Apparently her transformation was not as wonderful as she had imagined. She had expected him to enthuse as soon as he came in — but he appeared not to notice her changes. Well, she would not point them out . . . But she waited, glancing at him every now and again. Once he caught one of those expectant glances and asked, 'What's the matter? From the way you keep looking at me I might be exhibit A.'

She had been clearing the table and, about to replace the plate of bread-and-butter in the bread bin, she paused to ask, 'Shall I leave out all this after all?

You could have it for supper.'

'When we have just had such a colossal tuck-in!' he exclaimed. 'I'll want a drink but I'm sure I can't eat another crumb.'

Slowly, miserably, she finished clearing the table.

In the days which followed she knew Bill was different. He, who had sat unmoving in a chair for hours when they first came to London, was now unable to stay still for many minutes.

He would start to read a newspaper then, putting it down, walk restlessly to the window. Before long he would move across to the door and, without telling her where he was going, he would be off. Sometimes he was gone for only minutes, sometimes it would be hours.

Once Bertie had heard it said, '*Try* to hold on to a man and he'll feel smothered — that's the surest way to lose him.' So she said nothing and appeared not to notice his restiveness. But she was miserable. Only too well she was aware that he was no longer unhandsome. Yet he was not the Bill she had known in Cordery. His face had altered — and his eyes were different too. Never, never did they light now in amusement. Often she had been angry with him when he teased her. Now she wished he would, but he had, apparently, lost all his sense of humour.

She was clearing the table one evening when he stood up. She glanced at him, saw the way his eyes evaded hers, watched him when moments later he moved towards the door. She said abruptly, 'You don't ever want me to go out with you nowadays. Are you ashamed to be seen with me — me, the plain Jane?'

Bill halted and looked across at her, obvious surprise in his face. It was the first time Bertie had ever expressed anything of the rebellion which quite often welled up in her heart since his return.

'Ashamed?' He took the one word out of her sentence, and she saw the sudden distress in his eyes. 'No Bertie!

I wouldn't mind if I met the Queen when I was with you. I'd tell her you were the girl who brought me back to life — restored my belief in human nature. Bertie, you must believe me. I love you for all you have done for me. But sometimes I feel I must be alone.'

'All right, Bill. I'm sorry for blurting that out. I've never wanted to be possessive — only to help you.' She moved towards him. 'Bill, I want you to be happy — but you aren't, are you?'

'Yes I am — as happy as the next man.' He bent and put his lips against her cheek. 'Why shouldn't I be? Don't you fret about me, old pal.'

As he went away from her across the room he added, 'I won't be gone long.'

She watched the door close behind him. Then she went slowly to the window. She could hear the staccato echo of his steps on the street. Then there was nothing. She leaned her face against the glass. For the first time Bill had said, 'I love you.'

But such hollow words when nega-tived by the ones which followed — 'for what you have done.' Not for herself . . . Well, face it — she had failed. She had been so sure she could make him care.

But not any more could she hope. Bill did not *need* her now. Bill had his looks back — his looks but not yet his self-assurance. That was why he wanted to wander off alone . . .

The next evening he suggested, 'We'll go to the pictures.' And she knew he was remembering her last evening's outburst and trying to be kind. She began, 'No, Bill, not if . . . '

'Now then,' he interrupted, 'I'm not listening to any excuse. Off you go to get ready.'

The following afternoon he brought her in a bunch of flowers — but did not kiss her as he presented them.

And that night she lay rigidly in the bed beside him . . . waiting . . . as she had waited ever since his return from hospital. She heard his breath released in what sounded like a soft sigh. She knew he was not asleep. She laid her hand on his bare chest. She said in a low pleading voice, 'Bill . . . Oh, if you don't love me I can't help loving you . . . wanting you . . . '

He did not move and suddenly she felt she could not bear any longer being near him — fearing that he would not ever turn to her again. She clenched her fist and beat it several times against him. 'You'd be different if I was Marcia, wouldn't you? Yet what has she ever done for you?'

It was the first time Marcia had been mentioned between them since the beginning of their life together. He caught her two hands in his with a force that numbed her. 'Bertie, you don't know what you are saying. You can't know that just hearing her name turns and twists the valves of my heart. And — seeing her — has been — hell to remember.'

'Seeing her? Bill, when — when? You

mean lately — and you didn't tell me . . .'

'She was on the other side of the road — that night I had the accident. I forgot everything that had happened. I could see only *her*. I started to go towards her . . .'

'So, beyond everything else, she nearly killed you.'

'Don't say that — it was my fault.' There was agony in his low voice.

'Oh Bill, I'm sorry — but I do love you. Surely there is no need to tell you that — and it hurts me to know you are being hurt. Bill, I've tried all these months to make you forget. I want you to forget — now.' She began to run her fingers through his hair in the way he had always said he liked.

'That's something Marcia never did,' he said hoarsely and suddenly his hands on her were rough, his mouth found hers crushingly . . .

But in the morning she knew that had been a night to end all their nights together.

It was still dark but the luminous dial of her little bedside clock told her it was morning. Intermittently she had noted how the hours were creeping by. Bill had slept heavily beside her but she had remained awake. Now she got carefully out of bed, dressed, and went out — down the iron steps and along the pavement towards the phone box but, with her hand on the door, she drew back. It was too early.

She began to walk. It got gradually light. She saw the shine of ice in the gutters. She saw the icicles hanging from a low roof. But she was too frozen inside to feel the cold outside.

She did not know how long or how far she walked but at last she caught sight of the red of another phone box. Surely *now* it would not be too early. Slowly she let the door swing to behind her . . . lifted the receiver . . .

When she got back to the flat she found Bill shaved and dressed — ready for work. He looked at her. 'Bertie, where have you been? I was worried.'

Her glance went past him to the clock. 'Your breakfast,' she said, 'I must get it . . . '

'No, don't bother — I haven't time.'

To go to his work without breakfast. This had never happened before. 'Bill . . . ' She was wondering whether he would have felt relieved if he had found a note when he got up, saying she was gone for good.

He moved towards her. 'Bertie . . . ' And they were both remembering the night. He was regretting now the searing passion born of anger and frustrated longing. He might now have been trying to read what was behind Bertie's dark eyes, but her glance dropped and she turned away from him.

For a moment he stood looking at her. Then he said, 'I'll be late.' Seconds later he was gone.

That evening when Bill got home Bertie had made coffee and it was on a tray ready with two cups and saucers. She said, 'It will have to be fish and chips this evening. I'm just going to pop out for them.'

Bill sat down by the gas fire, reaching his hands towards the glowing bars. 'Gosh, it's cold out,' he said, and it was in the tone of someone speaking to a near-stranger. She said deliberately, 'About last night — and all the other nights — no one need ever know — nobody, remember that.'

He began to stand up. 'Bertie, what do you mean?'

'I'll only be a minute or two,' she called.

When she returned Bill was standing with his back to the fire. She pushed open the door and stepped inside the room. She was followed by someone else. Bertie moved towards the table and put down her packet of fish and chips.

But Bill did not see her. He was looking at the woman standing in the doorway. He said in a whisper, 'Marcia!'

Slowly the girl went towards him. He

put out his hands — eagerly but diffidently, like a child reaching for a glorious bubble that might disappear if touched. He said hoarsely, 'Marcia, have you come to torture me? Oh, I can't bear it — not just to see you and then — lose you again.'

Marcia's eyes were searching his face. 'No, Bill, I have come back for good. Bill . . . my dearest . . . I've missed you so much.'

With wide eyes Bertie had watched them. Torture — that was the word he had used . . . She saw Marcia's hands go out — then Bertie turned swiftly, quietly, away shutting the door noiselessly behind her. She took a case from the cupboard where she had placed it earlier in the day, and went down the iron steps for the last time.

In the street she turned. The railway station was not far away. When she reached the booking office she hesitated. She had to buy a ticket but where was she to go? It did not matter now. She said the first place that came into her mind — 'A single to Sotton.'

And as she turned away the word was tumbling chaotically through her mind. Sotton — where she had once watched Bill sail away from her . . .

She found the right platform, the right train, but all her movements were mechanical as though she was being guided by remote control. The only real thing was that two people were locked in one another's arms — back in the flat which *she* had shared with Bill and tonight . . . tonight . . .

By now Bill must know what she had meant by those last words she had spoken to him . . . probably the last words she would ever speak to him. That afternoon she had removed every trace of her own occupation. The bed was made and there was only one pillow on it, but tonight . . . tonight . . .

No, she must not think about tonight. Yet how could she go on living? Now that she had been wife to Bill, how could she go on without him? This was worse than when she had seen him go off to New Zealand.

She thought suddenly — why shouldn't *I* emigrate? If I made a new life for myself in a new country . . .

That was her solution. She would stay in Sotton till she could make her arrangements, then a brief trip home to see Dad and the children.

She found a corner seat in an empty compartment. The train was beginning to move and at the last moment a late-comer arrived, but Bertie did not glance round as the door was pulled back. She was gazing out of the window. The train jolted and began to gather speed.

'Bertie . . . '

Startled, she looked up. 'Dud!'

He moved towards her, sat down at her side.

'Fancy seeing you!' Stupid, trite words. 'But it can't really be happening. Dud, you . . . '

'I'm real enough,' he said in the gentle, well-remembered voice. 'I . . . I thought you . . . might need me so I came . . . '

'What do you mean? Why should you imagine I'd be needing you?'

'I met Mr. Fawley this morning. He told me about Bill and that Marcia had gone to him. I just had to come and find you.'

'But no one knew that I . . . ' She broke off.

'That you were with Bill . . . I knew.'

'How could you? I never gave any hint in either of my letters.'

'I knew you,' he said slowly. 'When I heard that Bill had been back and that he was in trouble — oh, it leaked out all right — that Bill was not a pretty sight and Marcia had turned against him. And I was sure why you had gone so suddenly. I knew you'd stick to him through thick and thin — for as long as he was a bird with an injured wing.'

She said huskily, 'You guessed that when the bird was better it would want to fly away from me.' All at once she was shaking with sobs. Dud looked down at her, his brown eyes filled with distress. Bertie was not the crying sort — he had never seen her cry before.

Awkwardly he put his arm round her shoulder and she burrowed her head into his jacket. Dud said nothing, just held her till the storm was over. Then, half-ashamed, she sat up dabbing at her eyes as she said, 'Dud, I've always longed for the things I wasn't meant to have. I so much wanted to be a teacher — and I can see now it wouldn't have been right for me. I wanted — Bill — and I got him — but it didn't bring me happiness. Oh Dud, I'm such a failure. I've decided I'll go abroad, but perhaps there I'd make just as big a mess of my life.'

'Why not m . . . marry m . . . me?'

'Marry *you*!' Bertie sat away from him a little, looking at him, seeing the hurt which leapt into his eyes at her exclamation. She said, 'I thought you and Eve . . . '

'Eve?' he repeated.

'I saw you one night — in your

greenhouse. I brought Joe to you . . . '
Stumblingly she spoke and Dud's
hands clenched over his knees as he
listened. When Bertie faltered to a stop
he said, 'You brought poor little Joe to
me. Why didn't you speak? Eve is
always gushing and enthusiastic — she
got very worked up about my cresset
stone. But she wouldn't fall in love with
an oaf like me. She is going to marry an
archaeologist.'

'Did she finish the book?'

'Yes.' His lop-sided grin came slowly.
'The cresset stone is in it — and
Cordery Abbey.'

'Oh Dud, you must be proud. What
did she write about you?'

'N . . . nothing. I didn't want to be in
a book . . . '

'But . . . ' Bertie began to protest
and then broke off. Of course Dud
would not want any sort of publicity,
but he *was* glad that his work had not
been in vain. He would be quietly
pleased when he saw Eve's pictures,
but he would *rather* she got the credit

for stone, ruins and all.

They travelled for some minutes in silence. Then Dud said, 'Bertie, you haven't answered what I asked you.'

She did not look at him. 'Dud, I couldn't do it. When you said you knew I had gone to Bill I thought you meant you knew I . . . lived with him.'

'That would make no difference to me,' he said in a low voice. 'I l . . . love you. I've w . . . waited for you. I don't want to go on waiting all my life. I'm n . . . not m . . . much of a hero but . . . but . . . '

'You are good and kind and faithful — what hero could be more than that?' Bertie put in quickly. 'It would be unfair of me to take advantage of your offer.'

'Do you want to take advantage of it or would you rather go to a country where you'd know nobody at all?' He grasped her hand and stroked it gently. 'Bertie, I'm like your bird with a broken wing, and so often you have been kind to me. I guess that's why I love you.

And I'll always be an injured bird — needing you. I won't ever want to fly away from you.'

'Oh . . . Dud . . . ' She looked up at him then. All at once she was really seeing his face for the first time the gentleness of his limpid eyes, the vulnerability of his mouth with those lips which could so easily betray him, the strength of his chin. It was not a handsome face, but one full of love and very lovable.

He was saying, 'My mother died a few weeks ago.'

'Oh — I didn't know.' There seemed nothing else for Bertie to say. To tell him she was sorry would perhaps not ring true. Mrs. Lambourne had always seemed a cold, stern woman — yet Dud must have cared for her . . .

It was almost as though he read her thoughts, for he said, 'She wasn't really my mother. I can just remember the misery and pain of the time just after my real mother left my father and went to live with another man who didn't want me. Perhaps his cruelty might in the end have killed me — only I was rescued . . . '

'By Mrs. Lambourne,' Bertie said.

'Yes, she was a mother and father to me — something my own parents never wanted to be.'

'I never guessed. To me she always seemed rather an ogre.'

'She wasn't — to me. But she was always fiercely possessive. She hated me to give my affection to anyone or anything except herself — that was really why she didn't like it when I took Joe home.'

'And why she seemed to dislike me,' Bertie suggested.

'She guessed what you meant to me. Bertie . . . ' All at once his arms went round her again and he bent his head towards her. His lips when they found hers were not at all hesitant, but as he drew away from her he faltered, 'N . . . now you w . . . will be angry w . . . with me?'

'No Dud. If you are willing to take

the risk — well, it's very comfortable to be loved — no, it's wonderful.'

'Risk?' he repeated. 'I don't think it is that. You may not know it — but I do . . . you've never been able to see the moon for the glare of the sun. But it's different — now.'

And she knew he was right. Bill had been the sun which blinded her and tingled her with disquieting heat, whereas the moon's rays would be gentle and very pleasant.

THE END